Where The World Going From Here

Where The Human Going From Here

Feeling The Future Pain

Schwab Murray and Dr. Charles R. Levin

Copyright© 2022 Schwab Murray and Dr. Charles R. Levin

Table Of Content

INTRODUCTION

The Human Journey

Humans are problem-solving creatures. We adapt both physically and psychologically in reaction to obstacles, allowing us to transcend our ancestors and intentionally progress. Throughout history, religious ideas have been linked to innovations and solutions. "As people's hardships and challenges have developed, so have their religious and ideological responses." We live among the ruins of once-effective solutions. They may become impediments to thinking and action if we ignore them. If we understand them, they are a treasure house that we can all enjoy. " From the oldest stone hammer to modern technologies, our ability to create and use tools determines our physical, mental, and social advancement. At each stage, we make decisions—for better or worse—that shape who we are and the difficulties we face.

If you want to increase your chances of having a significant positive impact on your career, we feel it's usually best to work on a worldwide issue that is massive in scale, solvable, and overlooked "**Where The World Going From Here**". These are not generally the world's biggest problems; rather, they are the issues that get little attention in relation to how important they are and how much can be done about them.

We are confronted with a reality that is vastly different from that of our forefathers. But we have the ability to comprehend and handle today's difficulties, many of which are man-made, if we first understand who we are and how the past has created us. We must recognize what is unchangeable in human nature and identify what we can and must actively change to ensure the future of ourselves and our planet.

The Human Trip is the trip of the human mind; how it developed, the environment it created, and the problems it faced; why and how it answered them; and how those solutions affected its development and subsequent acts.

Modern research has shown that traits that we thought were exclusive to the human brain are really shared by other species. Rats will give up food to help other rats, even strangers. Bonobos exhibit compassion and empathy, and many animals have a sense of justice.

Religion was supposed to be the source of morality, but morality is today recognized as an intrinsic trait in humans and other creatures. Previously hailed as providing a "ticket to paradise," virtues are now understood as evolutionary techniques for achieving the necessary "selflessness"—a selflessness that allows a more full awareness to settle in the brain. Our spiritual leaders and prophets, although usually misunderstood, all mentioned it. Our neurobiologists and evolutionary psychologists are now on board.

The human brain is adaptable. It has enabled humanity to adapt, survive, and even thrive all throughout the world. We are the only species capable of doing so. This flexibility, however, has a drawback: we are easily deceived and influenced by the group or community in which we find ourselves. We are social beings, designed to interact with others outside of our local circle, yet we frequently restrict ourselves to thinking in terms of "Us and Them."

Again, spiritual leaders, philosophers, and psychologists have noted this fact, most recently by scholar Idries Shah in the book Reflections:

"What was once a luxury, tolerance and attempting to understand others, has now become a need." This is because, unless we recognize that we and others are typically acting as we do because of instilled prejudices over which we have no control while assuming that they are our own beliefs, we may do something that will lead to our collective demise. Then we won't have time to figure out if tolerance is a good or a bad thing.

People are unable to confront prejudice because they are attempting to treat the symptom. The symptom is prejudice, and the cause is incorrect assumptions. "Assumption is the daughter of prejudice. "Most Westerners are unable to recreate this image because the Western brain is accustomed to transforming two-dimensional images into three-dimensional figures, preventing it from perceiving this image as it is.

Tolerance, foresight, liberality, and humility may now be regarded as essential prerequisites for our survival, as we are all one interconnected humanity. The dangers of ignoring this reality endanger our modern civilization, just as it did 3,000 years ago when the first interconnected global economy collapsed, ushering in a three-century Dark Age.

Today, we have the knowledge to avert what would otherwise be a much larger collapse. Because 75% of a human infant's brain develops outside in the world, we understand that our individual worlds are shaped by our families and culture, resulting in very different worldviews. That is one of the reasons why people from different cultures have such difficulty understanding one another: their visual systems are not the same. Nonetheless, these distinctions can no longer prevent us from addressing today's global issues.

Our human journey began more than 300,000 years ago, and understanding it will lead us to the next stage. One that is unmistakably human.

I'm not sure if everyone feels this way, but I'll be honest, as I always am, and I hope everyone will be as well. We often take our childhood experiences and transform them into character, but many things that are harmful to everyone are happening, and long ago, often with a sense of obligation to be mere bystanders, I heard the phrase "society is anesthetized," and I always imagined people literally taking forehead anesthesia when I heard it. I'll never know why we don't care about anything in our teens, or why we care too much about everything, but now that I'm 34 years old, with a four-year-old child, and I witness everything that has been happening on our planet, I couldn't keep these feelings any longer and needed to express them. We must act now, before the planet is destroyed and the boat captain seeks sanctuary on another planet, while the "useless" remain to drown with the ship. I am in the process of becoming a scientist, and as such, I am immensely worried about the direction of the world, as I am sure many others are. The world's largest corporations exploit it without regard for difference or concern; they simply require clean money, no matter how, and they endure little more than 100 years (so far), so if the world goes in 50 years, they are okay. Most people are unaware of the Earth's cycles and quirks. Wind, earth, fire, water, heart (the absence of which has resulted in rampant devastation), I am the captain of the planet, d--b? When you hear it in the animation, you simply assume that these are the components of the planet and that these are the important ones, but I didn't consider any other concerns, such as all of them being inextricably linked. Forests play critical roles in the environment, such as carbon fixation (CO_2), oxygen release into the atmosphere (O_2), hydrological cycle regulation, and many others. Did you know that a tree "throws" 1000 gallons of water into the sky every day? Most likely not. So, with the few remaining forests and hotspots on the planet, we won't be able to sustain life for long. So, what happens to our forests? How can we change this? What exactly is going on? We are "well" still on the earth, but soon we will not be, and what will happen to the following generations? It's OK if you don't worry about what happens once you die; life ends quickly and that's it; "it's over." But for those who care and want their children to live on a planet with a pleasant climate, clean water, and food free of pesticides that cause countless diseases, please feel invited and welcomed inside this blog, because I wish my daughter knew plants and animals, could swim in a natural lake, and eat toes, among other things. Sorry for the length of the text; I decided to end it because, aside from the fact that I lack writing skills and am not a Pasquale, I hope the text does not have many unpleasant flaws and is not tiresome. Thank you and a hug to everyone, and please feel free to interact with them.

"There will be strife as long as skin color is more important than glare in the eyes."

In the 2030s, the introduction of AI-based network topologies, paired with greater sensory digitization and breakthrough compression methods, shook the telecommunications industry.

Humans started to engage in long-distance hyper-experiential interactions in which all five senses were meticulously digitized. People have referred to it as teleportation until now, but the precise term, coined by a group of visionaries in the late 2010s, is "holographic telepresence."

During the early days of this technology, inevitable ego- and power-driven conflicts arose, but the universal sympathetic response generated by such a transparent, immersive, real-time multi-sensorial communications paradigm eventually allowed us to transcend cultural and socioeconomic boundaries across continents.

Meanwhile, advances in computer and neuro-science have provided people with sophisticated tools for measuring their own psychological states with the goal of increasing their well-being. This technology blossomed in the late 2030s, allowing humanity to achieve a higher level of collective consciousness. Along these lines, the last fundamental transformation before entering our era is the result of more disruptive technology breakthroughs in the 2040s.

This book also examines the new reality that has emerged in the aftermath of the coronavirus epidemic, asking what it implies for politics, economics, business, science, and culture. The book brings together studies by subject and contents to help mankind attain some success in the post-21st century. The World Ahead 2022 is the main magazine in our future-gazing brand, which also includes The World Ahead: What If? and The World Ahead: What If?

CHAPTER ONE

What is the future of the world in the next 300 years?

The world is in a constant state of motion; we are not where we were 300 years ago. Using WhatsApp Conversation, we envision what the world will be like in 300 years.

My prediction is that religion will lose its grip on people or that people will become more aware of the absurdity of some ideas as science expands the scope of what is conceivable.

Most genetic illnesses and diseases will be cured as a result of transhumanism, and people will live significantly longer lives.

However, if you believe we are not seeing eye to eye on some social issues, it will most likely be far worse.

"The youngsters today enjoy luxury; they have terrible manners, disdain for authority, exhibit disrespect for seniors, and prefer conversation to exercise." Children are now rulers rather than domestic employees."

That is a quotation from around 2400 years ago. not connected to technology, but the more dissimilar things seem, the more similar they are. I can only speculate on where parenting will be in 300 years. The line between good and wrong would have been blurred even more, nearly to nothingness.

Throughout the 2000s, I wondered where the hell the future we were promised was, and hoped it would hurry up and arrive. As we approach the 2020s, I'm hoping that everything slows down and stops trying to arrive all at once.

We're in for some interesting problems in the coming centuries, and I believe the next few centuries will be a watershed moment in human history. What happens during our lifetime will have a significant impact on the path humanity takes in the future. I hope we chose wisely.

Given the current ratio of intelligent to non-intelligent people, there will almost certainly have been a war of the century at that time, and rather than focusing on the growth of the planet, it will most likely have been about rebuilding and survival repercussions. With the path we're on, there will be massive changes in technology and climatic events. We are at odds with one another and with our planet.

The world's wealth will be concentrated in the hands of a few; this has always been the case, but it will become much clearer.

We greatly simplify the past because we will never truly appreciate or understand what it was like to live at the time. The agricultural revolution, urbanization, and the transition from hunter-gatherer to more sedentary existence may appear to us as an improvement and gradual development, but it would have been a significant change with enormous uncertainty. There are now numerous illnesses, infections, hazards, side effects, and more that come with this transition that people were not prepared for and may not understand.

The difference today is that, even though our technological and sociological changes are more rapid, we have the foresight to consider them and the knowledge to adapt to them.

We can discuss AI, privacy, automation, universal wages, climate change, and other issues while they are happening. We know these things are coming, and while they may be unknown and perplexing, we are far better prepared than we have ever been.

Anyway, I'm quite optimistic about the future. We are considerably safer, healthier, and more educated than in the past. It will be fascinating to see what the world will be like in 300 years.

How do you think the world will progress in technology over the next 300 years? We will most likely uncover a cure for certain types of incurable diseases. There would be several new technologies, and the government might conceal the possibility of time travel. In a nutshell, everything would change.

Our genetic aims would outweigh our safeguards. Artificial intelligence must not surpass humanity; else, it will be deadly. We cannot stop a world traveling at the speed of light, but we may attempt to solve it in other ways. We may protect the surrounding environment by planting trees or just avoiding harming it.

The change over the preceding 200–250 years has been profound. For thousands of years prior to the industrial revolution, established civilization was mostly agricultural, with 80–90% of humanity living in rural areas. Furthermore, capital accumulation was often much slower. Industrialization has created a world in which the main structural threat to the economy is underconsumption rather than a lack of supply. When

Adam Smith inferred a balanced equilibrium between supply and demand, I imagine he could scarcely comprehend the ludicrous production capabilities of present industrial technology.

The dynamics will be considerably more volatile in the next 300 years, with the globe becoming proportionately smaller as natural resources deplete and human resources expand. It will be difficult, but against popular belief, I will have faith in humanity's inherent ability to withstand whatever is thrown at it.

How The World Could

End

What Could Happen If the World Ends—and What We Can Do About It?

Rare cataclysms are difficult to predict and plan for, yet they may be too terrible to ignore.

The last family on Earth huddles around a fire, melting a pot of oxygen in a desolate apartment complex covered by layers of hanging rugs. The planet has been exiled to the cold outer reaches of the solar system after being ripped from the warmth of the sun by a rogue black star. The lone clan of survivors must go out into the never-ending night to collect frozen air gases that have accumulated like snow.

As far as end-of-the-world scenarios go, Fritz Leiber's 1951 short story "A Pail of Air" is a fairly implausible notion. Scholars who study such issues believe that a self-inflicted disaster, such as nuclear war or a bioengineered virus, is most likely to do us in. However, a range of other catastrophic natural catastrophes, including as threats from space and geological upheavals on Earth, might potentially disturb life as we know it, unravelling modern society, wiping off billions of people, or possibly eradicating our species.

Yet, according to Anders Sandberg, a catastrophe researcher at the University of Oxford's Future of Humanity Institute in the United Kingdom, there has been remarkably little research on the subject. "There are more studies about dung beetle reproduction than there are concerning human extinction," he says. "It's possible that our priorities are off."

Frequent, relatively catastrophic disasters, such as earthquakes, attract much more investment than low-probability apocalyptic disasters. Prejudice might also be at work; for example, scientists who pioneered studies on asteroid and comet impacts have complained about encountering a recurrent "giggle factor." Many academics, whether consciously or unconsciously, regard catastrophic risks as fiction or fantasy, rather than serious science, according to Sandberg.

HUMANITY THREAT

However, a few intellectuals continue to imagine the impossible. They claim that with enough information and sufficient preparation, it is possible to prepare for, and in some circumstances, avert, uncommon but deadly natural catastrophes. Giggle all you want, but the survival of human civilization may be jeopardized.

Solar storms are the first threat.

One threat to civilization may not be too little sun, as in Leiber's story, but too much. Bill Murtagh has seen how it may begin. On the morning of July 23, 2012, he sat in front of a colorful array of screens at the National Oceanic and Atmospheric Administration's Space Weather Prediction Center in Boulder, Colorado, watching twin clouds of energetic particles erupt from the sun and barrel into space, known as a coronal mass ejection (CME). After only 19 hours, the solar buckshot raced through the area where Earth had been only days before. Experts think that if it had hit us, we would still be in shock.

Murtagh now works as the assistant director of space weather at the White House Office of Science and Technology Policy in Washington, D.C., where he analyzes solar outbursts. CMEs do not directly harm humans, although their effects may be spectacular. They may cause geomagnetic storms that trigger spectacular auroral displays by funneling charged particles into Earth's magnetic field. However, powerful storms may generate lethal electrical currents in long-distance power lines. The currents last only a few minutes, but they have the potential to destroy electrical grids by shattering high-voltage transformers, especially at high latitudes where Earth's magnetic field lines converge as they arc toward the surface.

The worst CME event in recent history occurred in 1989, frying a transformer in New Jersey and knocking out power to 6 million people in Canada's Quebec province. The Carrington Event of 1859, named after the British astronomer who witnessed the accompanying solar flare, was up to ten times more intense. While the northern lights danced as far south as Cuba, they sent searing currents racing through telegraph cables, sparking fires and shocking operators.

"It was wonderful," recalls Patricia Reiff, a space physicist at Rice University in Houston, Texas. But if another storm of that magnitude attacked today's infrastructure, she adds, "there would be terrible ramifications."

Some experts fear that another Carrington-like disaster may destroy tens to hundreds of transformers, plunging vast parts of entire continents into the dark for weeks, months, perhaps even years, Murtagh said. That's because the custom-built, house-sized replacement transformers can't be bought off the shelf. Transformer producers claim that such fears are overblown and that most equipment will survive. But Thomas Overbye, an electrical engineer at the University of Illinois at Urbana-Champaign, says nobody knows for sure. "We don't have a lot of data related to major storms since they are relatively infrequent," he explains.

What is certain is that widespread blackouts might be disastrous, particularly in nations reliant on highly sophisticated electrical infrastructures. "We've done an excellent job of generating a significant vulnerability to this danger," Murtagh argues. Everything with a plug would be rendered unusable, including information technology, gasoline pipelines, water pumps, and ATMs. "That will have an impact on our ability to run the nation," Murtagh warns.

A significant event might happen in our lives. Carrington-like storms are thought to hit Earth once every few centuries, according to research; a recent analysis showed a 12% possibility that such a storm will occur in the next decade.

But at the very least, we'll see it coming. Solar telescopes detect CMEs as they originate, while spacecraft a million miles away assess important properties as they pass by. With information such as the direction of a CME's magnetic field, scientists may predict whether the particle cloud would flow around Earth like "a boulder in a river," or if the field will link with Earth's to cause a geomagnetic storm, according to Reiff. Forecasters may then send out notifications 30 minutes to an hour before the CME.

Such warnings are only meaningful if governments and grid operators are prepared to react, and nations all around the globe have only recently begun to take the issue seriously. The White House issued a thorough National Space Weather Strategy and an associated Action Plan last year, outlining the need to minimize risk and increase readiness. A bipartisan measure to make portions of the idea a reality will be introduced in the Senate shortly.

The electric grid is one of the plan's pillars. Operators have already begun inventorying vulnerable components and critical assets, prompted by regulatory authorities. The next step will be to protect the system by installing current-blocking devices such as series capacitors, which are becoming increasingly popular in the western United States because they improve long-distance power transmission, and by developing emergency protocols for regulating power loads to minimize transformer damage. According to Overbye, the electrical industry's quick response has been positive.

However, Overbye contends that full shielding against a Carrington-like disaster would be too expensive. Instead, in the event of an impending megastorm, operators may react by prematurely shutting down large portions of the system in order to protect transformers, thus embracing short-term damage in order to avoid a long-term disaster.

The second threat is cosmic collisions.

Another sky danger that must be avoided is a collision with a massive asteroid or comet. Experts believe that the only way for humanity to survive is to totally avoid the collision.

"That is something that we as a species must never, ever, ever allow to happen," Ed Lu says. "That is the end of humanity." Former astronaut Lu founded the B612 Foundation in Mill Valley, California, in 2002—a private organization dedicated to defending the globe against near-Earth objects, or NEOs.

Everyone has heard of the 10-kilometer-wide asteroid that helped wipe out the dinosaurs, but an asteroid a tenth of that size may end civilisation, according to Michael Rampino, an earth scientist at New York University in New York City. The collision site would be destroyed, and massive earthquakes and tsunamis would rip through the world. The long-term consequences, however, would be disastrous. Depending on the speed and angle of approach, a 1-kilometer-wide object could spit out enough fragmented rock to block out the sun for months. The haze would be exacerbated by soot from wildfires caused by debris falling back to Earth. "All of this material going back into the environment warms up, and it's like turning on your oven's broil setting," Rampino adds. When the smoke and dust combined, the earth would enter a so-called "impact winter," resulting in crop failures and catastrophic hunger.

Fortunately, asteroids of this size strike Earth about once every few million years, and "dino killers" about once every 100 million years. On an annual basis, your chances of dying from an impact are only slightly higher than those of dying in a shark attack, according to Mark Boslough, a physicist at Sandia National Laboratories in Albuquerque, New Mexico. However, just like sharks, it only takes one to pull the trick off.

As a result, NASA launched the Spaceguard survey in 1998, at the request of Congress. The goal was to recruit astronomers to detect 90% of the estimated 900+ NEOs larger than 1 kilometer in size, which the agency formally accomplished in 2010. Attempts are now underway to find any surviving giants and tag 90% of anything taller than 140 meters by 2020, but NASA estimates that they will fall short of their goal. None of the over 15,000 NEOs discovered so far are currently on a collision course with Earth. However, an Earth-bound NEO of significant magnitude will eventually meet civilisation in a disaster movie scenario. When that day comes, "it's going to shift from science fiction to scientific reality rather quickly," Lu predicts.

Science is already at work on the problem. In 2010, the US Geological Survey released Defending Planet Earth: Near-Earth Object Surveys and Hazard Mitigation Strategies. Given a few decades' notice, National

Research Council experts proposed various strategies for repelling an invader. We could ram it with a spaceship or two, gently alter its orbit with the gravitational pull of a spacecraft known as a gravity tractor, or blow it up with nuclear weapons.

Many concepts for planetary defense are currently only on paper, but others may see real-world testing in the coming decade. AIDA (Asteroid Impact and Deflection Assessment) is a collaborative mission planned by NASA, the European Space Agency, and other partners to test impactor technology on the asteroid Didymos, which will pass close to Earth in October 2022. NASA has also revealed plans to use an upgraded gravity tractor (in which the spacecraft removes material from the asteroid to increase its mass) on its Asteroid Redirect Mission, which was supposed to launch in 2021 but is currently facing funding issues. In the event of a genuine threat, many experts recommend a combination of these measures just to be safe.

However, when it comes to objects larger than one kilometer in diameter, as well as comets, which can appear unexpectedly, some experts believe nuclear power is the only solution. The idea is to shock the body rather than blow it up, which may cause more harm than good. Although the 1967 United Nations Outer Space Treaty expressly prohibits the deployment of nuclear weapons in space, scientists already have a basic understanding of the technology, and NASA and the Department of Energy launched a collaborative effort this year to refine its use against asteroids. Finally, NASA's Planetary Defense Coordination Office, which was established earlier this year, will determine when and how the US should respond to a potential impact.

The third threat is supervolcanoes.

The greatest chronic threat to our modern society, however, is domestic—and it strikes far more frequently than massive cosmic disasters. Every 100,000 years or so, a caldera up to 50 kilometers across collapses, ejecting mountains of magma. The resulting supervolcano is uncontrollable and disastrous. One such monster, the massive eruption of Mount Toba in Indonesia 74,000 years ago, may have wiped out most of humanity, creating a genetic bottleneck that remains in our DNA today—though this notion is contentious.

The ash cloak

A super-volcano is one that produces an explosive eruption of more than 450 cubic kilometers of magma—

roughly 50 times the size of Mount Tambora's eruption in Indonesia in 1815 and 500 times the size of Mount Pinatubo's eruption in the Philippines in 1991. Geologists can read the history of such explosions in layers of erupted material called tuff, and the geological record shows that super-volcanoes are repeat offenders. Toba, Yellowstone, the Long Valley Caldera in eastern California, the Taupo Volcanic Zone in New Zealand, and several places in the Andes are still active today.

None of these danger zones are currently a threat. In the event of another eruption, everything within a hundred kilometers of the crater would be killed, and ash would cover continents. A few millimeters of the chemical, according to Susanna Jenkins, a volcanologist at the University of Bristol in the United Kingdom, may harm crops; a meter or more can render land unusable for decades. Ash can also cause buildings to collapse, pollute water sources, clog electronics, bring planes to a halt, and irritate the lungs.

These localized effects can have far-reaching global consequences. Even a minor disruption in air travel caused by Iceland's Eyjafjallajökull eruption in 2010—far from a supervolcano—cost Kenyan farmers millions of dollars in lost revenue as perishable produce bound for Europe went to waste. "The more connected our society becomes, the more sensitive we are to anything, no matter how little, that happens on the other side of the world," says Hazel Rymer, a volcanologist at The Open University in Milton Keynes, U.K.

The most far-reaching effects, however, would be on the global temperature, which would be comparable to the effects of a major asteroid impact. Sulfate aerosols emitted by supereruptions may drop temperatures across much of the Earth by 5°C to 10°C for up to a decade, threatening global agriculture.

It's difficult to predict how bad things might be. "Volcano science is predicated on experience," says Ben Kennedy of the University of Canterbury in Christchurch, New Zealand, adding that scientists have never seen a supervolcano. Knowledge about minor eruptions might be useful, but it can also be misleading. Although supereruptions likely produce significant amounts of sulfate aerosols, according to Claudia Timmreck, a climate modeler at the Max Planck Institute for Meteorology in Hamburg, Germany, and others, the particles may be bigger and shower out quicker than those produced by lesser eruptions. Timmreck's team also discovered that the season in which a midlatitude volcano erupts, such as Yellowstone, impacts how far its emissions travel.

The most critical difficulties are potential warning signs. Researchers expect that a big eruption will be preceded by broad signs like earthquakes, increased outgassing, and ground deformation produced by rising magma. This interruption would probably begin months, if not years, in advance, allowing adequate time to evacuate people and create emergency response plans. Experts would struggle to choose when to enhance the warning, according to Jacob Lowenstern of the United States Geological Survey. The Geological Survey in Menlo Park, California, is in charge of the Yellowstone Volcano Observatory. "It will be difficult for scientists to persuade themselves simply because we only have a partial understanding of the complexities of the processes at work," he says.

Then there are the political stumbling blocks in responding to the threat. The 1985 Nevado del Ruiz eruption in Colombia killed 23,000 people, in part because the government ignored scientific forecasts. False alarms may be annoying at times. Authorities projected in the 1980s that geological instability would cause the Long Valley Caldera in California to erupt.

Although it did not, local real estate prices dropped, and the economy suffered as a consequence.

Experts must determine which indicators point to a catastrophic eruption rather than a minor one—or none at all. "We're pretty adept at finding precedents after the event," adds Rymer. Academics believe that, for the time being, the best option is to continue researching the plumbing that feeds volcanoes and to glean as much information as possible from minor future eruptions before the next supervolcano erupts.

Damage/fatalities by natural disaster type, as well as the number of reported disasters and expected deaths by natural disaster type, are graphed.

The fourth threat: what if it happens?

Finally, no amount of research can prevent or reduce supervolcanoes or other strange phenomena such as nearby supernova explosions or cosmic gamma ray blasts. The only way we can survive them is to have a backup plan. In such a strategy, the bottom line is food.

At least two scientists have already devised a strategy. In their 2015 book, Feeding Everyone No Matter What, David Denkenberger and Joshua Pearce present numerous strategies for feeding billions of people without using the sun.

Denkenberger, an architectural engineer at Tennessee State University in Nashville, became a disaster researcher a few years ago after discovering that mushrooms may have thrived during previous mass extinctions. "Why don't we just eat the mushrooms and avoid going extinct?" he wondered, wondering if humans had faced a similar quandary.

Individuals may grow mushrooms on leaf litter and tree stumps damaged by the disaster, according to Denkenberger. Even better would be to cultivate methane-digesting bacteria on natural gas feedstock or to convert the cellulose in plant biomass to sugar, which is currently used to produce biofuel. Denkenberger and Pearce, an engineering professor at Michigan Technological University in Houghton, believe that by adapting existing industrial units, survivors of the disaster could produce enough alternative foods to feed the world's population many times over.

Of course, infrastructure, international collaboration, and the rule of law must all remain. According to Seth Baum, executive director of the Global Catastrophic Risk Institute in New York City, a nonprofit think tank whose experts include Denkenberger, the unknown is whether human civilisation will survive or collapse.

"How would we perform?" According to Baum "I think the only sensible response one can give at this point is that we have no clue." To him, societal resilience in the aftermath of a disaster is just another issue for scientists to investigate, rather than leaving it to dystopian novelists and doomsday preppers.

He has no animus toward survivalists. "As ridiculous as they may appear on television, I'm actually relieved to know that others are out there doing such things," Baum says. "Hopefully it won't come to that," he adds quickly.

I've been skeptical (that you'll ever travel to the stars or buy a bunch of flying cars) and optimistic (that you'll live longer, get smarter, eliminate extreme poverty, and grow your own vegetables). But there's one thing I've always believed: there is a culture about which I could write. Our best guess is that, despite the impending disaster of climate change, essential continuity will continue for the next eight decades, at least in the way that allows these time capsules to exist.

Everyone has heard of the 10-kilometer-wide asteroid that helped wipe out the dinosaurs, but an asteroid a tenth of that size, according to Michael Rampino, an earth scientist at New York University in New York City, may destroy civilisation. Massive earthquakes and tsunamis would smash across the Earth, destroying the collision location. However, the long-term consequences would be disastrous. A 1-kilometer-wide asteroid might spit out enough smashed rock to block out the light for months, depending on the speed and angle of approach. Soot from wildfires caused by debris falling back to Earth would worsen the smog. "All of this material pouring back into the environment warms up, and it's like turning on the broil setting on your oven," Rampino explains. When the smoke and dust mixed, the planet would experience an impact winter, which would result in crop failures and widespread hunger.

Fortunately, asteroids of this size only strike Earth once every few million years, and "dino killers" only every 100 million. According to Mark Boslough, a physicist at Sandia National Laboratories in Albuquerque, New Mexico, your chances of dying from an impact are just slightly higher than those of dying in a shark attack on an annual basis. However, similar to sharks, it only takes one to pull off the trick.

As a consequence, at the request of Congress, NASA began the Spaceguard survey in 1998. The organization has achieved its aim of recruiting astronomers to discover 90% of the estimated 900+ NEOs greater than 1 kilometer in size in 2010. Efforts are presently ongoing to locate any remaining giants and tag 90% of all structures higher than 140 meters by 2020, but NASA believes they will fall short of their target. None of the over 15,000 NEOs discovered so far are currently on a collision course with Earth. However, a large Earth-bound NEO will ultimately strike civilization in a catastrophe movie scenario. When that day arrives, "it'll transition from science fiction to scientific reality very rapidly," Lu says.

Science is already working on the issue. Defending Planet Earth: Near-Earth Object Surveys and Hazard Mitigation Strategies was published by the US Geological Survey in 2010. Given a few decades' notice, National Research Council specialists offered a number of counter-intruder techniques. We could crash it with a couple of spaceships, gently modify its orbit with the gravitational pull of a gravity tractor, or blast it out with nuclear weapons.

Many planetary defense concepts are still on paper, while others may see real-world testing in the next decade. AIDA (Asteroid Impact and Deflection Assessment) is a NASA, European Space Agency, and other partners' collaboration project to test impactor technology on the asteroid Didymos, which will pass close to Earth in October 2022. NASA has also revealed plans to utilize an improved gravity tractor (a spacecraft that pulls material from the asteroid to increase its mass) on its Asteroid Redirect Mission, which was meant to launch in 2021 but is currently suffering from financing concerns. To remain secure in the case of a true danger, various experts propose a combination of these actions.

However, other experts feel that nuclear power is the sole option for objects greater than one kilometer in diameter, as well as comets that may arise unexpectedly. The idea is to shock the body as opposed to blowing it up, which may do more damage than benefit. Despite the fact that the 1967 United Nations Outer Space Treaty expressly prohibits the deployment of nuclear weapons in space, scientists already have a basic understanding of the technology, and NASA and the Department of Energy launched a collaborative effort this year to perfect its application against asteroids. Finally, NASA's Planetary Defense Coordination Office, formed earlier this year, will decide when and how the United States should react to a possible impact.

A caldera up to 50 km wide collapses every 100,000 years or so, ejecting mountains of magma. The resulting supervolcano is dangerous and unpredictable. One such monster, the massive eruption of Mount Toba in Indonesia 74,000 years ago, may have wiped out most of humanity, creating a genetic bottleneck that still exists in our DNA today—though this notion is debatable.

A supervolcano produces an explosive eruption of more than 450 cubic kilometers of magma, which is around 50 times the size of Mount Tambora's eruption in Indonesia in 1815 and 500 times the magnitude of Mount Pinatubo's eruption in the Philippines in 1991. Geologists can read the history of such eruptions in layers of erupted material known as tuff, and the geological record shows that supervolcanoes are repeat offenders. Toba, Yellowstone, the Long Valley Caldera in eastern California, New Zealand's Taupo Volcanic Zone, and other Andean locations are still active today.

Currently, none of these danger zones poses a threat. If another eruption occurred, everything within a hundred kilometers of the crater would be destroyed, and ash would blanket continents. According to Susanna Jenkins, a volcanologist at the University of Bristol in the United Kingdom, a few millimeters of the chemical may injure crops; a meter or more may leave land unusable for decades. Ash may also cause buildings to collapse, water sources to be contaminated, electronics to malfunction, aircraft to land, and irritate the lungs.

These localized impacts might have far-reaching global consequences. Even a slight interruption in air travel caused by Iceland's Eyjafjallajökull eruption in 2010, which was far from a supervolcano, cost Kenyan farmers millions of dollars in lost income as perishable commodities heading for Europe went to waste. "The more connected our society becomes, the more sensitive we are to everything, no matter how tiny," says Hazel Rymer, a volcanologist at The Open University in Milton Keynes, U.K.

However, the most far-reaching effects would be on global temperature, similar to the effects of a large asteroid impact. Sulfate aerosols emitted by supereruptions may drop world temperatures by 5°C to 10°C for up to a decade, threatening global agriculture.

It's difficult to predict how bad things will be. "Volcano research is predicated on experience," says Ben Kennedy of New Zealand's University of Canterbury, adding that scientists have never seen a supervolcano. Knowledge about minor eruptions might be useful, but it can also be misleading. Although supereruptions undoubtedly produce significant amounts of sulfate aerosols, Claudia Timmreck, a climate modeler at the Max Planck Institute for Meteorology in Hamburg, Germany, and others believe that the particles produced by supereruptions may be larger and shower out faster than those produced by minor eruptions. Timmreck's team also discovered that the season in which a midlatitude volcano, like Yellowstone, erupts has an influence on how far its emissions travel.

The most serious challenges are possible warning indicators. Researchers expect that a big eruption will be preceded by a broad range of signs, including earthquakes, increased outgassing, and ground deformation caused by rising magma. This interruption would very definitely begin months, if not years, in advance, giving plenty of time to evacuate people and establish emergency response plans. According to Jacob Lowenstern of the United States Geological Survey, experts would struggle to determine when to raise the alert level. The Yellowstone Volcano Observatory is managed by the Geological Survey in Menlo Park, California. "It will be difficult for scientists to convince themselves simply because we have a limited understanding of the complexities of the systems in action," he claims.

Then there are the political impediments to responding to the threat. The 1985 eruption of Colombia's Nevado del Ruiz killed 23,000 people, in part because the government disregarded scientific projections. False alarms may be annoying at times. Authorities predicted that geological instability will cause the Long Valley Caldera in California to erupt in the 1980s. Despite the fact that it did not, local real estate prices fell, and the economy suffered as a consequence.

Experts must assess if the indications point to a catastrophic eruption, a minor one, or none at all. "We're really good at finding precedents after the fact," Rymer adds. Academics believe that, for the time being, the best option is to continue researching the plumbing that feeds volcanoes and to gather as much information as possible from smaller future eruptions before the next supervolcano arises.

Damage/fatalities by natural disaster type are graphed, as are the number of recorded disasters and expected deaths by natural disaster type.

What if it happens? The fourth danger is

Finally, no amount of study can avoid or mitigate supervolcanoes or other unusual phenomena like nearby supernova explosions or cosmic gamma ray blasts. We can only withstand them if we have a backup plan. The bottom line in such a scheme is food.

An approach has already been offered by at least two scientists. In their 2015 book Feeding Everyone No Matter What, David Denkenberger and Joshua Pearce suggest numerous ways of feeding billions of people without using the sun in their 2015 book Feeding Everyone No Matter What.

Denkenberger, an architectural engineer at Tennessee State University in Nashville, became a disaster researcher after learning that mushrooms may have flourished through prior mass extinctions a few years ago. "Why don't we just eat the mushrooms and prevent becoming extinct?" he mused, wondering whether humans had ever faced a similar dilemma.

According to Denkenberger, individuals may grow mushrooms on leaf litter and tree stumps damaged by the calamity. Even better would be to cultivate methane-digesting bacteria using natural gas as a feedstock, or to convert plant biomass cellulose to sugar, which is currently used to produce biofuel. By adapting existing industrial units, Denkenberger and Pearce, an engineering professor at Michigan Technological University in Houghton, think that survivors of the calamity could generate enough alternative foods to feed the world's population many times over.

Infrastructure, international cooperation, and the rule of law must, of course, continue. The unknown is whether human civilisation will survive or collapse, according to Seth Baum, executive director of the Global Catastrophic Risk Institute in New York City, a nonprofit think tank whose specialists include Denkenberger.

"How would we fare?" Baum claims that "I believe the only reasonable reaction at this moment is that we have no idea." To him, societal resilience in the aftermath of a tragedy is merely another topic for scientists to research, rather than leaving it to dystopian authors and doomsday preppers.

He has no ill will against survivalists. As absurd as they may seem on television, I'm truly happy to hear that similar thing are going on, "Baum says. "Hopefully, it won't come to that," he immediately adds.

Are you getting me?

I've been skeptical at times (that you'll ever travel to the stars or buy a bunch of flying cars) and optimistic at others (that you'll live longer, get smarter, eradicate extreme poverty, and produce your own veg). But I've always imagined that there is a culture about which I might write. Our best guess is that essential continuity will continue, despite the coming disaster of climate change, at least for the next eight decades, at least in the manner that allows these time capsules to exist.

Nonetheless, it is always worthwhile to re-examine our assumptions, especially when the future is at stake. Nobody wants to seem like a soothsayer in hindsight. As strange as it may seem, my correspondents, I must question your existence. I confess, I do it all the time, because of one recurrent response to these letters from my contemporaries: How do you know there will even be a 22nd century?

My generation is one in which catastrophic fears are never far from the surface; maybe yours is as well. Perhaps it's just our nature to constantly predict our horrific demise. In my childhood, I developed an odd fascination with the possible end of the world. I grew up in the 1980s, beneath the twin shadows of the Cold War and Chernobyl, and in the early 1990s, my nuclear-phobia gave way to climate-phobia. Pandemics entered my nightmare cycle in 1995 with the films Outbreak and 12 Monkeys; asteroid collisions entered my nightmare cycle in 1998 with Deep Impact and Armageddon.

Then 9/11 happened, and I saw a shattered nation lose its mind for years. The United States wasted billions of dollars and thousands of lives fighting a perceived threat that turned out to be insignificant. (Every year, far more Americans are killed by unsecured furniture than by terrorists.) My impulse was to write about the true civilization-ending risks I'd long feared, in order to rectify the balance in the media, which, according to one study, was overrepresenting terrorism as a cause of death by a factor of 4,000.

But every time I did, I learned that my worst end-of-the-world scenarios had also been exaggerated—and that was before we launched a pandemic that, although horrifying and terribly disruptive, would likely kill much less than 0.1 percent of the world's 7.8 billion people.

Climate change can and will do much worse, but try finding a climate scientist who believes it will completely destroy civilization even in our worst-case scenario for your century. (Which, by the way, is improving as we continue to make little improvements in the right direction.)

What about asteroids? We've monitored everything in the area that may wipe us out, and the only one with a 0.3 percent chance of hitting us won't arrive until 2880. (I'll keep it in mind for my next series, "Dear 29th Century.")

Why is this not more well known? Why did various news outlets just last month advertise the threat of an asteroid that will never come close to Earth? Why was a 2018 international scientific research study that said we needed to reduce carbon emissions by 45% by 2030 and achieve net zero by 2050 turned into "climate change will kill the globe in 12 years" panic headlines by media organizations that should know better? (At the time of the flurry of publications, one Washington lobbyist noted that the same senators who had previously resisted climate change on Capitol Hill were now justifying the delay because "the world is ending anyhow."

Why? Because of something more dangerous than the troubles themselves: the attitude author Rebecca Solnit refers to as "naive cynicism." Even in the face of evidence that activism works (say, shutting down a single oil pipeline), many people in my day seem to have a preemptive "It's all wrecked, so why try" mentality. "The return to failure is a defensive strategy," Solnit argues. "In the end, naive cynicism is a method for turning away from the always imperfect, sometimes important triumphs that life on Earth provides—and for lumping everything together regardless of size," says the author.

So, for the rest of this, let us analyze the risks that may, in theory, wipe out humanity on a large scale. But, like we should have done with terrorism, we should keep our sense of scale in mind, and remember that science and ingenuity can and have fended off a lot of genuine threats to our species in the past. Here are the existential threats, listed in reverse order of their likelihood of killing billions before the end of the twenty-first century.

1. Asteria

Deep Impact and Armageddon have company in the minds of moviegoers as of late 2021. Don't Look Up, Adam McKay's comedy, depicts a celestial body speeding towards Earth and a disintegrating society that can't get its act together to believe it or care enough. It was received as intended by the director, as a metaphor for our current epidemic of basic scientific denial. However, the metaphor choice was ironic; humanity has done an excellent job of quietly watching massive objects and their orbits during the last few decades. We can cross the extinction-level asteroid threat off our list for many decades to come, thanks in large part to NASA's Spaceguard Survey. In 2018, astronomer Michael Busch informed me, "We've identified everything out there that's more than 1 kilometer broad." "Anything less than a kilometer would simply result in a regional disaster."

That's not to say we shouldn't look up. We absolutely must! There are several rocks out there that might devastate a huge populated area. The next frontier for telescopic watchers is to identify all of the 100-meter-plus wide city-killers. The biggest reported impact, a 1908 blast that devastated 500,000 acres of Siberian woods, is now thought to have been caused by a 200-meter-diameter asteroid or comet. We locate around 3,000 of these babies each year, and a new NASA monitoring system predicts an increase in that number, so we should have them all tagged by the time you arrive. You're really welcome.

We're really good at orbital mathematics, and there's a lot of empty space out there, so we can be certain that Elon Musk's small space bound Tesla Roadster won't collide with any planet for the next million years. Concerns about a 10-kilometer rock like the one that killed the dinosaurs — well, they belong with the dinosaurs, as far as you and I are concerned.

2. **Pandemics**

As I speculated after HBO Max's series, Station Eleven may be the ultimate great pandemic-ends-the-world scenario. Even the novel's author, Emily St. John Mandel, has admitted that her hypothetical sickness could not spread in the way she envisioned. The virus "would have burned out before it could take off the whole population," Mandel observed calmly as COVID-19 began its perilous journey around the globe.

While we may expect further pandemics in mine and your century, Mandel's was accurate. Viruses seem to have a difficult evolutionary route to follow. They can be extremely lethal, like Ebola, with a 50% fatality rate, and kill their hosts before they can spread far and wide, or they can be relatively mild and infect millions of hosts, like COVID-19 and its mutations, which is much more effective at causing "long COVID" damage (which one paper estimates in the region of 100 million cases so far, or nearly a quarter of total infections), and crippling our healthcare systems, than in ac (5.67 million deaths and counting.)

It's difficult for a virus to kill quickly if it also wants to propagate. Continuous human invasion into the natural environment is not unthinkable; like the 1918-9 pandemic, which likely started on a pig farm in Kansas that was on the flight route for migrating birds, it was not unthinkable (like the 1918-9 pandemic, which likely began on a pig farm in Kansas that was on the flight path for migratory birds). Even if a virus wins the mutation lottery, say by coupling strict deadlines with a 30-day incubation period, it still needs to contend with a more cunning human race.

Just look at what we did to slow COVID-19: In 2020, an unprecedented amount of masking and social distancing saved millions of lives in 2020 (compare to 1918, when San Francisco was one of the few cities to try a mask mandate, and authorities failed to keep it in place), followed by the rapid development of safe and effective vaccines. Then, in one year, the largest health campaign in history completely vaccinated half of the world. There was shocking unfairness in distribution (much of Africa will remain without immunization doses until 2023), as well as astonishing success stories (Brazil is currently more vaccinated than the United States, owing to our old acquaintance the universal healthcare system) (Brazil is now more vaccinated than the U.S., thanks to our old friend the universal healthcare system).

Regardless, the whole world is on high alert. When the next epidemic occurs, whether in my lifetime or yours, the human race will be ready. Our medical community is currently debating how to correct the errors and institutional shortcomings shown by COVID. We're investigating what worked and what didn't with COVAX, a well-intended, first-of-its-kind global effort to offer immunizations to disadvantaged countries. We hope that by the first pandemic of your century, vaccine hoarding by wealthy nations is the norm. Who knows, maybe you'll even convince the scientifically deficient minority that a little "research," especially from online swindlers, is dangerous.

3. Population expansion

I arrived too late for the 1970s population growth scare. It was inspired by the 1972 book The Limits of Growth, which predicted that humanity would reach the limit of human resources by the twenty-first century and was highly criticized for using an insanely pessimistic computer model. Regardless, the research sold like crazy—you'll never go bankrupt anticipating the end of the world as we know it—and it remains a foggy background issue for the 2020s' naive cynics.

Since Thomas Malthus, an 18th century thinker who advocated for the forcible sterilization of the poor, population prophets have predicted doom. Thanos, the villain in multiple Marvel films (remember those?), has a similarly ominous demeanor. However, Malthusian worries about too many mouths to feed were never realized since agriculture has always kept up. As it did during the Green Revolution, which quadrupled agricultural output throughout the globe, the Limits of Growth team was entering inaccurate statistics into its computers at the same time. With 7.8 billion people, we are still not living in the overpopulated Soylent Green cannibalistic apocalypse prophesied for this year.

While the world's population continues to rise, its rate is decreasing-so much so that our forecast for the number of individuals on the earth in your century is being revised lower. (Our current best prediction is somewhere between 10 and 11 billion, with a steady decrease after that.) Birth rates are falling all around the globe as a result of urbanization and women's education. According to the UN, half of the world's population already lives in countries with fertility rates lower than the replacement rate.

What about the opposite worry, that reproduction rates might plummet to zero all at once, as in the Children of Men scenario? I admire that image as much as everyone else, but it was a work of fiction primarily intended to depict the treatment of immigrants during the war on terror. It was set in 2027 and it was believed that the youngest human on Earth was born in 2009 for reasons that were kept deliberately undisclosed. The Y chromosome is certainly in jeopardy, but not by much; we'll probably be stuck with it for the next four million years or so. If a catastrophic reproductive crisis occurs in our or your century, there should be enough egg and sperm banks and IVF operations to get us through it.

4. nuclear conflict

I still have nightmares about the alleged four-minute gap between the sirens' roar and missiles reaching Newcastle, the nearest important city to where I grew up in the UK. Would my 12-mile-away home survive the first blast? And if it did, would we regret it? The answer was reinforced throughout the 1980s by horrifying television pictures such as Threads and The Day After:

indeed, the aftereffects of nuclear war are many. The living would gradually become envious of the dead. And this was before we knew anything about the "nuclear winter" that would cover the world in ash, perhaps causing long-term famine for years.

During the Cold War, the United States and the Soviet Union each had up to 70,000 nuclear weapons. Since then, many treaties, most notably the new START treaty of 2021, have helped reduce the global total to 13,000, with the United States and Russia controlling all but a thousand of them. This would have seemed like an impossible utopia when I was a kid, back when every prediction for the twenty-first century predicted that at least a few nukes would have been exploded in anger by now.

To be clear, there are still far too many nuclear weapons, enough to wipe out civilization many times over if they were all deployed simultaneously. We still have much too much launch authority concentrated in far too few hands, which kept me up from January 2017 to January 2021. But the world survived a US president who had to continually ask his generals why he shouldn't contemplate deploying nukes for anything (even battling an impending storm) (including attacking an incoming hurricane). Even Donald Trump was held in check when it came to conflict by the philosophy of Mutual Assured Destruction.

Will that doctrine last into the twenty-first century? Will North Korea use its weapons on the spur of the moment? Will India and Pakistan go to war? Will the United States, Russia, or China send birds soaring, maybe with Ukraine or Taiwan as flashpoints? Your life is entirely dependent on the leaders of nuclear-armed countries and everyone in their lines of command, who realize in their bones that even a minor exchange may kill us all. We survived Trump in the twenty-first century. We may not be so fortunate the next time.

In other words, each generation may need to shoot its own threads to ensure it never happens again. Continuous nuclear nightmares for all of us would be a dreadful, but maybe necessary, side effect.

5. Climate change

In a recent letter, I explored the dangers of what you may call The Catastrophe. So, I won't dwell too long on the floods, famines, droughts, wildfires, polar vortexes, billions of climate refugees by mid-century, and "wet bulb" heatwaves that fry the internal organs of anybody unlucky enough to live without air conditioning. This and other consequences of our inability to reduce carbon emissions quickly enough may be recent history to you.

Or maybe not. Because, here's the thing about our ongoing bout of global weirdness: we can still restrict its effects. In The Uninhabitable Earth: A Story of the Future, a typically pessimistic summary of the science, "We will always have the power to make our next decade better or worse than the previous one

We're already making strides toward increasing renewables and decreasing our reliance on fossil fuels. Just a few years ago, the number of climate commitments from nations and corporations specifying 2035 as a target date for complete decarbonization would have been unthinkable. Despite the fact that emissions have not yet peaked, our creaking supertanker of a civilization has started to shift in the right direction.

It is now too late to prevent climate change from deteriorating in the 2030s. Perhaps it's too late for the 2040s. But our efforts today might make life easier in the 2050s and beyond, lessening the need for future authorities to sanction some dangerous mitigation plans, such as polluting the upper atmosphere to reflect more of the sun's rays.

Our climate modelling seems to be convergent on a three-degree Celsius increase by the end of the century. Insignificant or not, I'm not going to sugar-coat the possibility that a billion or more people may die as a result of its direct and indirect effects in the meanwhile. (Already, particle pollution caused by fossil fuels kills up to 8.7 million people per year.)

Even if spread out over a century, a billion deaths would be horrifying. By far the worst calamity in history. One that, sooner or later, will need our globe to mobilize on a scale not seen since World War II, should be avoided and curtailed at all costs. (Calling it a "war on warming" makes more sense than a "war on terror.")

Is it, however, an existential threat to human civilization? When scientists are directly asked this question, they reply "no." Even science fiction's most ardent climate change campaigner, Kim Stanley Robinson, envisions a day when we adjust our motivations to make carbon sequestration economically possible for rich and poor alike—through the use of a carbon cryptocurrency.

6. Crisis escalation

Other once-in-a-blue-moon hazards to humanity are on the horizon. The supervolcano under Yellowstone might erupt without warning, engulfing most of North America in ash, reducing temperatures and rainfall and perhaps destroying the rainforests. A massive magnetic solar flare from the sun at the wrong time might knock down electricity networks all around the world, causing unimaginable devastation. Or Earth may be hit by a gamma-ray burst from a nearby star, which causes DNA damage and may have caused earlier mass extinctions.

These are all probable unusual occurrences, but we don't know how rare they are in each instance. (The most terrifying may be the solar flare phenomenon, which last happened in 1859.) It's only a roll of the cosmic dice whether it happens in my century or yours.

But there's one more kind of end-of-the-world scenario to consider. What if many of the events mentioned in this letter occur concurrently?

It has commonly been said that a city-leveling asteroid strike during the Cold War may have been misinterpreted as a nuclear attack, sparking a global conflagration between the superpowers. It is not beyond the realms of possibility to imagine a bioengineered bug, a war, and a worldwide drought all happening concurrently. Or for one of them to set off a chain reaction of bad outcomes that tears civilisation apart. Living in the midst of a COVID-caused supply-chain crisis makes such scenarios seem all too likely.

"I've always thought' single failure 'apocalypse stories were unsophisticated, underrating our civilization's tremendous endurance," science fiction writer David Brin responded to my Station Eleven view. I'd whittled down the idea of his linked book, The Postman, to a post-nuclear apocalyptic scenario. Indeed, as Brin pointed out, nuclear war only killed 70% of the Postman world's inhabitants.

However, it devastates our deeply competent institutions, leaving us vulnerable to a triple whammy of subsequent blows-disease and climate chaos-and finally onslaught by waves of ultra-right-wing militias bent on recreating feudalism—what the worst males have always done in difficult times." The fact that it would take all four to destroy everything was crucial.

Consider one conceivable cascading disaster, and you may see one wherever you look. Then you have to question yourself to what extent you've loaded the dice in the service of a peculiar need to assume the worst. Would a single catastrophe, or even a series of tragedies, genuinely bring out the worst in people, to the point that this interwoven web we call civilisation, this decentralized information network seemingly designed to resist nuclear war, would vanish in a vast savage sweep?

A Paradise Built in Hell, Rebecca Solnit's account of what occurs after tragedies like the 1906 San Francisco earthquake, 9/11, and Hurricane Katrina makes a more persuasive case. People bond together more for survival and comfort in each case, not less. For the length of the crisis, a form of utopian culture arises. No money changed hands, as it did in 1906 in San Francisco, when the wealthy and poor cheerfully brushed shoulders at soup kitchens in Golden Gate Park, and the only gunshots occurred when troops mistook civilians clearing the wreckage as looters.

So, in the face of these impending storms, this is my daring forecast. The more our issues worsen, the more human compassion and inventiveness will emerge. We shall follow the ancient programming revealed in The Dawn of Everything, 2021's most significant book, and join together in tribes for mutual help. The internet will continue to function, although at a reduced capacity, thanks to our ever-increasing supply of solar and wind energy. Without the crap we've piled on top of civilization, it may seem more real than ever.

Still, here's hoping we never have to find out the truth. Cascading disasters are something I would not want for my worst future adversary.

CHAPTER TWO

THE WORLD IN 20 YEARS

Looking at population statistics can help us assess the promise and challenges of the coming decades.

"Demographics determine fate."

It is a saying typically attributed to the French philosopher Auguste Comte that says that the relatively simple trend lines of populations foretell much of the future. Do you want to know how the power dynamic between the US and China will alter over the next 20 years? An economist would advise you to examine both countries' demographics. (China's economy is expected to surpass that of the United States by 2028, although it will stay smaller per capita.)

Do you want to know how much lithium we'll need to mine over the next 20 years to create batteries? The solution will most likely be provided by demographics. (According to the International Energy Agency, we will need 13 to 42 times the amount we currently consume.) And so forth.

Forecasting the future could be a fool's errand. However, commercial and political leaders do not use demographic statistics to assess the potential and difficulties of the next two decades. We're all too focused on the present moment, the next quarter, and the next year.

Of course, demographics are incapable of detecting pandemics or other natural disasters. However, as shocking as it may feel at the time, such occurrences are uncommon.

When Dk began publishing 20 years ago, following 9/11, forecasters predicted that travel would be reduced indefinitely. True, air travel was altered permanently after the attacks, but development in air travel was back on pace within months. Why? Demographics More people around the world have more disposable income and are increasingly seeking to live closer to cities with greater access to airports. This, combined with the human tendency to like being with other people, makes forecasting certain aspects of the future almost mathematical.

Technological developments are one part of the future that demography cannot anticipate. However, even technical advancements have a slower impact on daily life than we sometimes realize. In 2013, Peter Thiel famously stated, "We wanted flying automobiles." Instead, we were given 140 characters. "

So, what's next? What would be different if you awoke 20 years from today in 2041? Here are some data-driven recommendations that don't require a crystal ball.

According to UN projections, metropolitan areas will house over 70% of the global population by 2050.

That means that most cities will require extra infrastructure. Roads, public transportation, and waste management will all require significant expansion and renovation. The average person generates 4.9 pounds of garbage each day, up from 3.66 pounds in 1980. However, as a result of technological advancements, there is a trend in the opposite direction: According to the US Environmental Protection Agency, paper and paperboard use decreased from 87.7 million tons in 2000 to 67.4 million tons in 2018.

We'll also demand a lot more energy.

Based on population growth and consumption patterns, the United States will require around 28% more energy in 2040 than it did in 2015. On our current trajectory, approximately 42% of electricity in the United States will come from renewable sources.

Where will that energy be generated? Elon Musk predicted five years ago that solar energy could be generated on mostly unpopulated land masses and transported to population centers. He described China as having "a great geographical breadth, the majority of which is hardly populated at all," adding that the majority of the country's people live in coastal cities. "With solar, you could easily power all of China."

On-demand everything is another trend that, like growing energy consumption, isn't new and isn't going away. We have come to expect goods and services to be delivered at the push of a button, often within minutes.

This could have an impact on real estate, particularly retail space in cities. As firms strive for faster deliveries, they will need to warehouse products closer to customers. Real estate investors are already planning to build mini-warehouses on every block. Furthermore, urban population density is expected to alter food production and distribution. Vertical farming—under indoor, regulated conditions—may move from the vision of certain start-ups to a new reality in order to deliver fresh food to clients quickly.

And we'll be older by then. According to the United Nations, we will live to be 82.4 years old in the United States, up from the present life expectancy of 79.1 years. That's great news for healthcare providers and others who serve the elderly. However, living three more years is likely to be more expensive, which will have an impact on both working and saving. Official forecasts, according to the Urban Institute, "expect 2.1 employees per Social Security claimant in 2040, down from 3.7 in 1970." Entrepreneurs, industry leaders, and policymakers are already working to solve some of the problems that demographic data suggests are ahead of us, whether it's figuring out how to incentivize farmers to sequester carbon, using insurance as a tool to reduce coal production, reinventing heavy industry motors to use less energy, or writing laws to help govern code.

What about the interconnected universe? Or how about cryptography? Or are robots taking our jobs? Or will A.I. take over everything? Such questions cannot be answered by demographics. All of that could happen, but life in 2041 could look a lot like it does now – with the exception of those flying cars.

IDEAS ABOUT TO

CHANGE OUR WORLD

Future technology: 22 concepts ready to impact our planet. The future is coming, and sooner than you think. These coming technologies will revolutionize the way we live, how we care for our bodies and help us prevent a climate calamity.

Whether you like it or not, technology is continuously advancing, delivering new ideas and ground breaking initiatives every year. Some of the absolute brightest minds are out there designing the next piece of futuristic technology that will fundamentally revolutionize how we live our lives. It might seem like scientific advancement is stable yet we have lived through a time of great technical growth in the previous half century.

There are breakthroughs occurring right now that are plucked directly from the pages of science fiction. Whether it be robots that can read minds, AI that can produce pictures on their own, holograms, bionic eyes, or other mind-blowing technologies, there is a lot to anticipate from the realm of future technology. We've chosen some of the largest and most fascinating concepts.

Sand batteries

Not every invention bettering our future needs to be difficult. Some are basic but incredibly successful.

One of these sorts of inventions has emerged from some Finnish engineers who have developed a technique to transform sand into a big battery.

These engineers put 100 tons of sand into a 4 x 7-metre steel container. All of this sand was then heated up using wind and sun energy.

This heat may then be supplied by a local energy provider to offer warmth to buildings in adjacent locations. Energy may be stored this way for lengthy periods of time.

All of this happens via a concept known as resistive heating. This is when a substance is heated by the friction of electrical currents.

Sand and any other non-super conductor are warmed by the electricity travelling through them, creating heat that may be utilized for energy.

Underwater gloves

Plenty of technical breakthroughs have originated from mimicking the features of animals, and the 'octa gloves' are no exception.

Researchers at Virginia Tech have built underwater gloves that imitate the suction ability of an octopus for a human hand.

The scientists behind these gloves re-imagined the way that an octopus's suckers operate. This design was intended to fulfill the same purpose as the mentioned suckers, namely, to initiate an attachment to items with little pressure.

Through the use of these suckers and an array of micro-sensors, the suckers on the gloves are able to tighten and loosen to grab items underwater without delivering a crushing force.

This might be utilized in the future for rescue divers, underwater archaeologists, bridge engineers, salvage personnel, and other comparable professions.

Xenotransplantation

Inserting the heart of a pig into a human seems like a poor idea, and yet, this is one of the newest medical operations that is witnessing tremendous development.

Xenotransplantation—the practice of transplanting, installing or infusing a person with cells, tissues or organs from an animal source—has the potential to change surgery.

One of the most popular operations conducted so far is the implantation of a pig's heart into a person. This has now successfully occurred twice. However, one of the patients was only alive for a few months, while the second is currently being examined.

In these procedures, the heart cannot be directly transplanted into a person; gene-editing has to take place beforehand. Certain genes need to be knocked out of the heart and human genes need to be introduced, primarily surrounding immunological acceptance and genes that inhibit excessive development of heart tissue.

At present, these procedures are hazardous, and there is no surety about their success. However, in the near future, we might see xenotransplants occurring on a daily basis, transferring hearts or tissues from animals to people in need of them.

AI image-generation

As artificial intelligence continues to do occupations just as effectively as humans, there is a new sector to add to the list—the realm of art. Researchers at the firm OpenAI have devised a program that is able to make graphics with merely written cues.

Type in "a dog wearing a cowboy hat singing in the rain" and you'll receive a plethora of wholly unique photographs that meet that description. You can also specify the type of art that will be returned in response to your request. However, the technology isn't finished and still has flaws, as when we gave it inadequate suggestions on developing cartoon characters.

This technology, known as Dall-E, is now in its second version and the team behind it wants to continue developing it further. In the future, we may see this technology utilized to establish art exhibits, for corporations to generate rapid, creative graphics, or, of course, to alter the way we make memes on the internet.

No longer a science fiction stereotype, the application of brain reading technology has increased considerably in recent years. One of the most fascinating and practical applications we've seen so far comes from researchers at the Swiss Federal Institute of Technology Lausanne (EPFL) (EPFL).

Thanks to a machine-learning algorithm, a robot arm, and a brain-computer interface, these researchers have succeeded in establishing a way for tetraplegic patients (those who can't move their upper or lower body) to interact with the environment.

In testing, the robot arm would do basic tasks like navigating around an obstruction. The system would then analyze data from the brain using an EEG cap and automatically decide whether the arm had performed a motion that the brain regarded as inappropriate, for example, moving too near to the obstacle or traveling too rapidly.

Over time, the system may then adapt to the person's preferences and brain signals. In the future, this might lead to wheelchairs controlled by the brain or support equipment for tetraplegic patients.

3D-printed bones

3D printing is an industry offering anything from inexpensive home construction through to affordable robust armour, but one of the most exciting applications of the technology is the manufacturing of 3D printed bones.

The company Ossiform specialises in medical 3D printing, creating patient-specific replacements of different bones from tricalcium phosphate – a material with similar properties to human bones.

Using these 3D-printed bones is surprisingly easy. A hospital can perform an MRI, which is then sent to Ossiform, who creates a 3D model of the patient-specific implant that is needed. The surgeon approves the design and then, after it is produced, it may be utilized in surgery.

What is special about these 3D printed bones is that, because of the use of tricalcium phosphate, the body will remodel the implants into vascularised bone. That means they will enable the full restoration of function that the bone it is replacing had. To ensure the greatest integration possible, the implants are of porous nature and have extensive holes and channels for cells to adhere to and rebuild bone.

Realistic holographs

Holograms have been populating science fiction literature, films, and society for years now, and although they do, they do exist, they remain they remain a tough thing to produce, particularly on a wide scale. However, a hypothetical technology that might alter this is holobricks.

Developed by academics from the University of Cambridge and Disney Research, holobricks are a means of tiling together several holograms to generate a huge, seamless 3D picture.

The difficulty with most sholograms right now is the quantity of data that they require to generate, particularly when done on a large scale. A standard HD display for a 2D picture needs roughly 3GB per second to develop. A hologram of comparable size and quality would be close to 3TB per,second, which is a large amount of data.

To overcome this, holobricks would supply discrete pieces of one huge holographic picture, substantially lowering the amount of data required. This might ultimately lead to the employment of holograms in regular consumer, entertainment, including movies, games, and digital displays.

Clothes that you can hear

Wearable technology has grown leaps and bounds over the years, introducing new functionality to the items and apparel we wear day to-day. One possible possibility is giving garments ears, or at least the same capability as an ear.

Researchers at MIT have created a fabric that is able to detect a heartbeat, handclaps, or even very faint sounds. The scientists claimed that this may be employed in employed in wearable gear for the blind, utilized in structures to detect fractures or stresses, or even weaved into fishnets to detect the sound of fish.

For now, the material used is thick and a work in progress, but they hope to roll it out for consumer use over the next few years.

Lab-made dairy products

You've heard of cultured "meat" and Wagyu steaks made cell by cell in a laboratory, but what about other animal-based foodstuffs? A growing number of biotech companies around the world are investigating lab-made dairy products dairy products, including milk, ice-cream, cheese, and eggs. And more than one believes they've cracked it.

The dairy sector is not ecologically friendly, not even close. It accounts for 4% of global carbon emissions, more than air travel and shipping combined, and demand for a greener splash to pour into our tea cups and cereal bowls is growing.

Milk is not as difficult to produce in a laboratory as meat. Rather than generating it from stem cells, most researchers want to synthesize it via fermentation, thus producing the milk proteins whey and casein. Some products, such as Perfect Day's, are now available in the United States, with ongoing efforts aimed at replicating the mouthfeel and nutritional benefits of traditional cow's milk.

In addition, researchers are developing lab-grown mozzarella that melts correctly on top of a pizza, as well as other cheeses and ice cream.

Planes powered by hydrogen

The World Future Versus Science

When it comes to commercial airplanes, carbon emissions are a major concern, but there is a viable solution that has received substantial funding.

The ideas for a hydrogen-powered aircraft were presented as part of a £15 million UK effort. Fly Zero is a project conducted by the Aerospace Technology Institute in collaboration with the UK government.

The group has developed a concept for a mid-size aircraft powered entirely by liquid hydrogen. It would be able to transport 279 passengers halfway around the world without stopping.

If this technology becomes a reality, it might mean a zero-carbon trip with no stops between London and Western America or a single stop between London and New Zealand.

Digital "twins" that keep track of your health

Q Bio's Dashboard

Q Bio's dashboard, where customers may check their health

Humans may go into the medbay in Star Trek, where many of our ideas about future technology arose, and have their whole bodies digitally checked for indicators of disease and injury. In practice, the inventors of Q Bio say that doing so will improve health outcomes while relieving strain on clinicians.

US businesses have created a scanner that can check hundreds of markers in about an hour, ranging from hormone levels to fat accumulation in your liver to signals of inflammation or any number of cancers. It intends to use this information to create a 3D digital avatar of a patient's body, known as a digital twin, that can be tracked throughout time and updated with each new scan.

According to Q Bio CEO Jeff Kaditz, it will usher in a new era of preventive, tailored care in which the massive amounts of data gathered will not only help physicians prioritize which patients need to be seen right away, but will also be used to develop more sophisticated methods of detecting illness. Here's an interview with him.

Direct air capture

Trees, via the process of photosynthesis, have remained one of the most effective ways to reduce CO2 levels in the atmosphere. However, emerging technologies may achieve the same goal as trees by collecting more carbon dioxide while taking up less space.

Direct Air Capture (DAC) is the name given to this approach (DAC). It entails capturing carbon dioxide from the atmosphere and either storing it in deep geological caverns beneath the earth or combining it with hydrogen to create synthetic fuels.

While this technology has great potential, it is currently beset by a number of challenges. There are now operational direct air capture plants, although the current versions need a large amount of energy to function. If energy levels can be reduced in the future, DAC might be one of the most significant technological achievements for the environment's future.

"Green Burials"

People confronting the realities of climate change are prioritizing sustainable living, but what about eco-friendly dying? Death is often a carbon-intensive process, leaving a last impression of our ecological footprint. A normal cremation, for example, is said to emit 400kg of carbon dioxide into the atmosphere. So, what is a more environmentally friendly option?

Instead, you could be composting in Washington State, USA. Bodies are placed in chambers that contain bark, mud, straw, and other things that aid in natural decomposition. Your corpse gets changed to soil after 30 days and may be returned to a garden or forest. According to Recompose, the method uses one-eighth of the carbon dioxide produced by cremation.

Fungus is used in an alternative method. Luke Perry, the late actor, was buried in a custom "mushroom suit" developed by a start-up named Coeio in 2019. According to the company, its suit is made of mushrooms and other microorganisms that aid in decomposition and combat toxins that are detected when a person normally decays.

Most alternative methods of disposing of human bodies after death are not based on new technology; they are just awaiting societal acceptance. Another example is alkaline hydrolysis, which involves breaking down the body into its chemical components over the course of six hours in a pressurized chamber. It is legal in some US jurisdictions and produces fewer emissions than more traditional methods.

Artificial vision

For decades, bionic eyes have been a staple of science fiction, but real-world research is now catching up with far-sighted authors. A spate of new technologies are on the horizon that will help individuals with different sorts of visual impairments regain their sight.

In January 2021, Israeli physicians implanted the world's first artificial cornea into a 78-year-old man who was blind on both sides. When his bandages were removed, the patient was able to immediately read and recognize family members. The implant also naturally attaches to human tissue without being rejected by the recipient's body.

In 2020, Belgian scientists created an artificial iris linked to smart contact lenses that address a variety of vision disorders. Scientists are even developing wireless brain implants that bypass the eyes entirely.

Montash University in Australia is conducting trials for a system in which users wear a pair of glasses connected to a camera. This sends data directly to the implant, which is located on the surface of the brain and provides the user with a rudimentary sense of sight.

Bricks for energy storage

Scientists have discovered a method for storing energy in the red bricks used in building construction.

Researchers led by Washington University in St Louis in Missouri, US, have developed a method that can convert the affordable and widely available building material into "smart bricks" that can store energy like a battery.

Although the research is still in its early stages, the researchers think that walls made of these bricks "may store a substantial quantity of energy" and can "be recharged hundreds of thousands of times within an hour."

Scientists from Washington University in St. Louis invented a red brick gizmo that lights up a green light-emitting diode (D'Arcy laboratory: Washington University in St. Louis).

Scientists at Washington University in St. Louis devised a red brick gizmo that lights up a green light-emitting diode. D'Arcy Laboratory/Washington University in St. Louis

The researchers found a method to convert red bricks into a kind of energy storage device known as a supercapacitor.

This entailed adding a conducting coating known as Pedot to brick samples, which then seeped through the porous nature of the charred bricks, changing them into "energy storage electrodes."

The researchers stated that iron oxide, which is the red tint of the bricks, assisted in the process.

Smartwatches are powered by sweat.

Engineers at the University of Glasgow have developed a unique kind of flexible supercapacitor that stores energy by replacing the electrolytes found in regular batteries with sweat.

It may be fully charged with as little as 20 microlitres of fluid and is strong enough to withstand 4,000 cycles of the kind of flexes and bends it may encounter in use.

The device acts by coating a polyester cellulose fabric in a thin layer of a polymer that serves as the supercapacitor's electrode.

As the fabric absorbs the perspiration of its user, the positive and negative ions in the sweat interact with the polymer's surface, resulting in an electrochemical process that generates energy.

Smartwatches are powered by sweat.

"Conventional batteries are cheaper and more abundant than ever before, but they are frequently constructed with unsustainable materials that are harmful to the environment." Professor Ravinder Dahiya, director of the University of Glasgow's James Watt School of Engineering's Bendable Electronics and Sensing Technologies (Best) group, agrees.

"This makes them difficult to safely dispose of and potentially harmful in wearable devices, where a broken battery might spill dangerous contents on the skin."

"What we've done for the first time is demonstrate that human sweat has the true capacity to completely eliminate those hazardous components while providing excellent charging and discharging performance."

'Living concrete' that heals itself

Scientists created what they call "living concrete" by combining sand, gel, and microorganisms.

According to the researchers, this building material has structural load-bearing capabilities, is self-healing, and is more environmentally friendly than concrete, which is the second most-consumed resource on Earth after water.

The University of Colorado Boulder team believes their research opens the path for future building construction that can "repair their own fractures, suck up harmful chemicals from the air, or even light on command."

Living robots

Tiny hybrid robots produced from frog embryo stem cells might one day float through human bodies to particular places in need of medication or collect microplastic in the sea.

"These are innovative living devices," said Joshua Bongard, a computer scientist and robotics specialist at the University of Vermont who collaborated on the development of the millimetre-wide bots known as xenobots.

"They are neither a typical robot nor a recognized kind of animal." It's a brand-new kind of artifact: a living, programmed organism. "

Everyone can use the internet.

Even though we can't seem to live without the internet (how else would you read sciencefocus.com?), only around half of the world's population is online. There are a variety of reasons for this, including economic and social issues, but for others, the internet is simply unavailable due to a lack of connectivity.

While Google is gradually addressing the issue by using helium balloons to beam internet to inaccessible areas, Facebook has abandoned plans to do the same with drones, allowing firms such as Hiber to steal a march. They've taken a different approach, sending their own network of shoebox-sized microsatellites into low Earth orbit, which wakes up a modem connected to your computer or device as they fly by and transfer your data.

Their satellites orbit the Earth 16 times per day and are already being used by organizations like the British Antarctic Survey to provide internet access to the most remote parts of our world.

Future green technology

Where is my flying automobile, dude? 11 future innovations that we have yet to see

Future green technology that is exciting

Sound may drown out forest fires.

Forest fires may one day be extinguished by robotic drones that emit loud noises into the trees below. Because sound is made up of pressure waves, it may be used to upset the air surrounding a fire, cutting off the oxygen supply to the fuel. The fire simply goes out at the proper frequency, as researchers at George Mason University in Virginia recently demonstrated with their sonic extinguisher. Bass frequencies seem to be the most effective.

Fast-charging of electric vehicles is seen as critical to their adoption, with motorists able to stop at a service station and entirely charge their vehicle in the time it takes to have a coffee and use the restroom – a little longer than a regular break.

However, specialists at Penn State University in the United States fear that rapid charging of lithium-ion batteries may destroy the cells. This is due to the fact that the movement of lithium particles known as ions from one electrode to another in order to charge the unit and keep the energy available for use does not occur smoothly while charging at low temperatures.

Scientists recently discovered that if the batteries could be heated to 60 °C for just 10 minutes and then swiftly cooled to ambient temperatures, lithium spikes would be avoided and heat damage would be avoided.

The battery design they developed is self-heating, with a thin nickel foil producing an electrical circuit that heats in less than 30 seconds to warm the inside of the battery. The cooling system built inside the car would be used to provide the fast cooling necessary while the battery is charged.

Their study, which was published in the journal Joule, proved that they could charge an electric automobile entirely in 10 minutes.

Silicon chips with artificial neurons

Scientists have found a method for implanting artificial neurons onto silicon chips, duplicating the neurons in the human nervous system and their electrical properties.

"Until now, neurons were like black boxes, but we were able to open the black box and see inside," said University of Bath Professor Alain Nogaret, who conducted the experiment.

"Our research is paradigm-shifting because it provides a consistent method for precisely replicating the electrical properties of actual neurons."

However, it's wider than that, since our neurons only need 140 nanowatts of power. That's one billionth the power consumption of a microprocessor, which was previously used in attempts to build synthetic neurons.

CHAPTER THREE

THE FUTURE IS AI

The AI Future: How Will Artificial Intelligence Alter Reality? AI is constantly changing our environment. Here are a few examples of how AI will impact our lives.

"Think simple" is the guiding principle for every AI. The phrases are written in simple font on a scrap of paper and pinned to the back upstairs wall of their industrial two-story workplace. But what they're doing with artificial intelligence is anything but easy.

Gyongyosi throws up hazy video footage of a forklift driver running his vehicle in a warehouse while sitting at his messy desk, snuggled near an oft-used ping-pong table and prototypes of drones from his undergraduate days hanging overhead. It was captured from above by a Onetrack.AI "forklift vision system."

The Future Of Artificial Intelligence

Artificial intelligence is altering the human future in almost every industry. It is already a fundamental driver of emerging technologies such as big data, robotics, and IoT, and it will remain a technological pioneer for the foreseeable future.

The shoebox-sized device detects and categorizes countless "safety events" using machine learning and computer vision. It doesn't see everything, but it sees a lot. Such as the direction the driver is looking while driving, how swiftly he is travelling, where he is going, the locations of the people around him, and how other forklift operators are operating their trucks. IFM's software detects safety violations, such as cell phone use, and alerts warehouse managers so they may take appropriate action. The primary goals are to prevent accidents and increase efficiency. Gyongyosi feels that the mere fact that one of IFM's devices is watching has had "a tremendous influence."

"If you think about it in terms of a camera, it really has the richest sensor accessible to us today at a very exciting price point," he says. "Because of smartphones, cameras and image sensors have become incredibly inexpensive, yet we collect a large amount of data." We may be able to infer 25 signals from a photo today, but in six months we will be able to infer 100 or 150 signals from the same image. The only difference is the program that examines the image... Every client may benefit from every other customer we get on board because our systems begin to watch and comprehend more processes and find more critical and relevant items.

MORE ON AI'S FUTURE

CAN AI MAKE ART MORE HUMAN?

The AI Evolution

FM is only one of numerous AI innovators in a field that is still expanding. For example, 2,300 of IBM inventors' 9,130 patents granted in 2021 were AI-related. Elon Musk, the founder of Tesla and a tech tycoon, has pledged $10 million to fund ongoing research at the non-profit research organization OpenAI—a drop in the metaphorical bucket if his $1 billion co-pledge in 2015 is any indication.

After several decades of intermittent hibernation throughout an evolutionary phase that began with "knowledge engineering," technology progressed to model-and algorithm-based machine learning, with a growing emphasis on perception, reasoning, and generalization. Now, AI has reclaimed center stage like never before — and it's not going away anytime soon.

WHAT IS THE IMPORTANCE OF ARTIFICIAL INTELLIGENCE?

AI is crucial because it is the foundation of computer learning. Computers have the capacity to harness massive amounts of data and use their learned intelligence to make optimal decisions and discoveries in fractions of the time that humans would take.

What industries will be affected by AI?

There is hardly any field that contemporary AI hasn't already touched. More specifically, "narrow AI," which performs objective tasks using data-trained models and typically falls into the categories of deep learning or machine learning, this has been especially true in recent years, as data collection and analysis have grown substantially as a result of ubiquitous IoT connectivity, the proliferation of connected devices, and ever-faster computer processing.

Some industries are just getting started with AI, while others are seasoned travellers. Both have a long road ahead of them. Regardless, the influence of AI on our daily lives is difficult to deny.

Transportation: Although it may take some time to develop, self-driving automobiles will one day transport us from place to place.

Manufacturing: AI-powered robots collaborate with people to execute restricted tasks such as assembling and stacking, while predictive analytical sensors keep equipment working properly.

Healthcare: Diseases are more quickly and reliably diagnosed, medication development is sped up and simplified, virtual nursing assistants monitor patients, and big data analysis helps to provide a more tailored patient experience in the comparably AI-nascent sector of healthcare.

Education: AI is being used to digitize textbooks, early-stage virtual tutors aid human teachers, and face analysis assesses students' emotions to help discern who is struggling or bored and better adapt the experience to their unique requirements.

Journalism is also using AI and will continue to gain from it. Bloomberg employs Cyborg technology to aid with the comprehension of complicated financial reporting. The Associated Press uses Automated Insights' natural language capabilities to publish 3,700 earnings report articles every year, approximately four times more than in the past.

Last but not least, Google is developing an AI assistant that can conduct human-like calls to arrange appointments at, say, your local hair salon. The computer understands context and nuance in addition to words.

However, these and other enhancements are just the beginning. There will be lots more to come.

"I think anybody making assumptions about intelligent software's capabilities peaking at some point is wrong," says David Vandegrift, CTO and co-founder of the customer relationship management company 4Degrees.

Big things are bound to happen with companies spending billions of dollars on AI products and services each year; tech titans like Google, Apple, Microsoft, and Amazon spending billions to create those products and services; universities making AI a more prominent part of their curricula; and the US Department of Defense upping its AI game. Others are well on their way to becoming a reality; others are merely hypothetical and may remain so. All are disruptive, for better or worse, and there is no sign of a slowdown in sight.

"A lot of industries go through this cycle of winter, winter, and then an eternal spring," Andrew Ng, former Google Brain chief and Baidu top scientist, told ZDNet. "We may be in the eternal spring of AI."

THE SOCIAL IMPACT OF AI

During a discussion at Northwestern University, AI researcher Kai-Fu Lee defended AI technology and its potential impact while simultaneously conceding its drawbacks and limitations. He cautioned against the former.

"The poorest 90 percent of the world, notably the lowest 50 percent in terms of income or education, will be severely impacted by employment displacement... The simple question is, 'How routine is a job?' And that is how likely it is that a job will be replaced by AI, since AI may learn to optimize itself within the context of everyday employment. And the more quantifiable the activity, the more objective it is—separating stuff into bins, washing dishes, picking fruits, and answering customer service inquiries are all extremely programmed, repetitive, and regular tasks. They will be replaced by AI in five, ten, or fifteen years.

Selecting and packing chores are still done by humans in Amazon's warehouses, which are buzzing with more than 100,000 robots — but that will change.

Lee's viewpoint has recently been mirrored by Infosys president Mohit Joshi, who told the New York Times, "People are going for extraordinarily large statistics." Previously, they had set modest personnel reduction targets of five to ten percent. They're now saying, 'Why can't we do it with 1% of the personnel we have?'"

On a brighter note, Lee emphasized that today's AI is useless in two ways: it lacks originality and it has no capacity for compassion or love. It is, rather, "a device to enhance human creativity." What is his solution? Those in jobs that demand repetitive or regular activities must learn new skills to avoid being left behind. Amazon even pays its employees to train for jobs at other companies.

"One of the absolute prerequisites for AI to be successful in many [areas] is that we invest tremendously in education to retrain people for new jobs," says Klara Nahrstedt, a computer science professor and director of the Coordinated Science Laboratory at the University of Illinois at Urbana-Champaign.

She is concerned that this is not happening widely or regularly enough. Gyongyosi by IFM is much more thorough.

"People need to learn about programming at the same time they learn a new language," he says, "and they need to do it as soon as possible because it really is the future." If you don't know how to write or program, it will just become more difficult in the future.

And, although many people who are displaced by technology may find new jobs, Vandegrift believes this will take time. American culture, like the country's change from an agricultural to an industrial economy during the Industrial Revolution, played a significant role in causing the Great Depression. However, the short-term impact was strong.

"The transition between jobs disappearing and new ones arising," Vandegrift continues, "is not often as pleasant as people like to assume."

Mike Mendelson, a learner experience designer at NVIDIA, instructs in a different manner than Nahrstedt. He works with developers who want to learn more about AI and use their knowledge in their businesses.

"If they understand what the technology is capable of and the domain incredibly well, they start to make links and say, 'Maybe this is an AI problem, maybe that's an AI problem,'" he says. "That is more prevalent than 'I have a specific problem I want to tackle.'

IN THE NEAR FUTURE

Some of the most intriguing AI research and experimentation, in Mendelson's opinion, is taking place in two areas: "reinforcement" learning, which deals in rewards and punishment rather than labeled data; and generative adversarial networks (GAN), which allow computer algorithms to create rather than simply assess by pitting two nets against each other. The former is demonstrated by Google DeepMind's Alpha Go Zero's Go-playing ability, while the latter is represented by unique image or audio output based on learning about a certain subject, such as celebrities or a specific type of music.

On a far larger scale, AI is expected to have a significant impact on sustainability, climate change, and environmental issues. City life will become less congested, less polluted, and more liveable, ideally and largely via the deployment of smart sensors.

"Once you foresee anything," Nahrstedt says, "you may dictate certain laws and rules." Sensors on cars that transmit data about traffic conditions might, for example, predict potential problems and enhance traffic flow. "By no means is this perfected," she confesses. "It's still in its infancy, but it will play a significant role in the future."

WILL ARTIFICIAL INTELLIGENCE TAKE OVER THE WORLD?

AI is expected to have a long-term impact on almost every industry, with 60% of firms affected. We already see artificial intelligence in our smart devices, autos, healthcare systems, and favorite apps, and its effects will continue to permeate many more areas in the near future.

RISKS FROM AI AND PRIVACY

Of course, much has been made of the fact that AI's reliance on vast amounts of data is already causing major damage to privacy. Look no farther than Cambridge Analytica's Facebook misbehavior or Amazon's Alexa eavesdropping, just two examples of technology gone wild. Opponents argue that without sufficient rules and self-imposed limitations, the situation would worsen. In 2015, Apple CEO Tim Cook chastised competitors Google and Facebook for greed-driven data collection.

"They're consuming whatever they can find out about you and trying to market it," he said in a 2015 speech. "We feel that is incorrect."

Cook later elaborated on his concerns at a talk in Brussels, Belgium.

"Advancing AI by amassing enormous human profiles is a kind of laziness, not efficiency," he said. In order for artificial intelligence to be really intelligent, it must respect human values, especially privacy. " If we do this wrong, the consequences will be severe."

Many others concur. According to a 2018 study conducted by the UK-based human rights and privacy NGOs Article 19 and Privacy International, fear of AI is limited to its everyday activities rather than a catastrophic shift such as the arrival of robot overlords.

"AI can improve society if used correctly," the experts added. However, as with most new technology, there is a major risk that commercial and governmental use may have a negative impact on human rights.

The authors concede that gathering massive amounts of data might be used to foresee future behavior in benign ways, such as spam filters and recommendation engines. However, there is a risk that it may jeopardize personal privacy and the right to be free from discrimination.

Getting Ready for the Future of AI

ARTIFICIAL GENERAL INTELLIGENCE'S POSSIBILITI

In late 2018, Stuart Russell, a prominent AI researcher, joked (or not) about his "formal deal with journalists that I won't talk to them unless they pledge not to include a Terminator robot in the piece." His remark expressed a clear dislike for Hollywood depictions of far-future AI, which tend to be overdone and scary. What Russell refers to as "human-level AI," sometimes known as artificial general intelligence, has long been a source of inspiration for science fiction.

However, the chances of that happening anytime soon, if at all, are slim.

"There are still significant breakthroughs that must occur before we get anything like human-level AI," Russell remarked.

Russell also said that AI is not yet capable of fully comprehending English. This is a significant difference between humans and AI at the moment: people can interpret and grasp machine language, but AI cannot do the same for human language. However, once AI has mastered human languages, AI systems will be able to read and comprehend everything ever written.

"Once we have that capability, you could query all of human knowledge and it would be able to synthesize and integrate and answer questions that no human being has ever been able to answer because they haven't read and been able to put together and join the dots between things that have remained separate throughout history," Russell added.

Science Time Video:

This gives us enough to think about. On that note, recreating the human brain is very difficult, which is another argument for AGI's still-speculative future. John Laird, a long-time University of Michigan engineering and computer science professor, has been researching the subject for decades.

"The goal has always been to construct what we call the cognitive architecture, which we feel is crucial to an intelligence system," he adds of his work, which is heavily inspired by human psychology. One thing we know, for example, is that the human brain is not just a homogenous collection of neurons. There is a genuine structure in terms of numerous components, some of which are tied to knowledge of how to do things in the real world."

This is known as procedural memory. Then there's information based on general facts, also known as semantic memory, and knowledge based on previous experiences (or personal facts), known as episodic memory. One of Laird's studies includes teaching a robot fundamental games like Tic-Tac-Toe and riddles using natural language instructions. These instructions often include a description of the goal, a list of permissible motions, and a list of failure scenarios. The directives are internalized by the robot and used to coordinate its activity. However, breakthroughs are sometimes slow to emerge — maybe slower than Laird and his colleagues would want.

"Every time we make progress," he continues, "we have a new appreciation for how difficult it is."

Is AGI A DANGER TO HUMANITY?

More than a few top AI experts believe (some more fervently than others) in a nightmarish scenario in which superintelligent robots take over and irreversibly change human life via slavery or annihilation.

The late theoretical physicist Stephen Hawking famously proposed that if AI starts to build better AI than human programmers, the end result might be "machines whose intellect surpasses ours by more than ours exceeds that of snails." Elon Musk believes and has warned that artificial intelligence is humanity's biggest existential threat. Attempts to bring it about, he claims, are akin to "summoning the monster." He has even expressed concern that his friend, Google co-founder Larry Page, may unintentionally steer something "evil" into existence despite his best efforts. Consider "a fleet of artificial intelligence-enhanced robots capable of eradicating humanity." Even IFM's Gyongyosi, who is not an alarmist when it comes to AI projections, does not rule anything out. He adds that at some point, individuals will no longer need to be taught systems; they will learn and evolve on their own.

"I don't think the tactics we're using now in these areas will result in computers deciding to kill us," he says. "I think that in five or ten years, I'll have to reevaluate that comment because we'll have other technology and methods to go about these things."

While lethal robots may remain science fiction, many think they will supplant humans in other ways.

The Future of Humanity Institute at Oxford University presented the results of an AI survey. The paper is titled "When Will AI Outperform Human Performance?" "Evidence from AI Specialists" includes predictions for AI's future development from 352 machine learning experts.

This category had a large number of optimists. A median number of respondents predicted that by 2026, robots would be capable of writing school essays; by 2027, self-driving vehicles would render drivers obsolete; by 2031, AI would outperform humans in the retail sector; by 2049, AI could be the next Stephen King; and by 2053, the next Charlie Teo. The somewhat scary climax is that by 2137, all human labor will be automated. But what about the individuals themselves? No probably sipping umbrella drinks served by droids.

Diego Klabjan, a Northwestern University professor and the original director of the school's Master of Science in Analytics program, considers himself an AGI skeptic.

"At the moment, computers can handle somewhat more than 10,000 words," he explains. "A few million neurons, then." However, human brains have billions of neurons that are linked in a very fascinating and sophisticated manner, while the current state-of-the-art [technology] is just plain connections that follow rather simple patterns. So, I don't envision expanding from a few million neurons to billions of neurons with present hardware and software technologies.

How will AGI BE USED?

Klabjan also has little faith in extreme possibilities, such as vicious cyborgs that turn the earth into a fiery hellscape. He's much more concerned about machines—such as combat robots—being given incorrect "incentives" by unscrupulous individuals. In a 2018 TED Talk, MIT physics professor and notable AI researcher Max Tegmark said, "The fundamental risk from AI isn't malice, as in stupid Hollywood movies, but competence—AI achieving goals that simply aren't aligned with ours." That's also Laird's point of view.

"I don't see a circumstance where something wakes up and decides it wants to take over the planet," he continues. "I feel that's science fiction, and it's not going to happen."

What Laird is most concerned about is "evil individuals exploiting AI as a type of phony force multiplier" for crimes such as bank robbery and credit card fraud, among many others. As a result, although he is sometimes unhappy with the pace of progress, AI's slow burn may really be a positive.

"Time to understand what we're producing and how we're going to integrate it into society," Laird continues, "may be just what we need."

But no one knows for certain.

"There are many crucial breakthroughs that must occur, and they may come very fast," Russell said during his Westminster speech. In reference to British scientist Ernest Rutherford's discovery of the quick transformative impact of nuclear fission (atom splitting) in 1917, he said, "It's very, very difficult to foresee when these conceptual breakthroughs are going to happen."

But, if and if they do, he emphasizes the need for planning. This includes beginning or ongoing conversations concerning the ethical use of AGI and whether or not it should be controlled. That includes striving to reduce data bias, which corrupts algorithms and is now a thorn in the AI ointment. This necessitates working to develop and improve security systems capable of keeping technology under control. And it takes humility to recognize that simply because we can, does not mean we should.

"Most AGI specialists predict AGI within decades, and if we just bumble into this unprepared, it would most likely be the worst mistake in human history." In his TED Talk, Tegmark stated, "It may allow for brutal global dictatorship with unprecedented inequality, monitoring, misery, and, maybe, human extinction." However, if we steer carefully, we may end up in a glorious future in which everyone is better off—the poor are wealthier, the wealthy are richer, and everyone is healthier and free to pursue their goals."

ARTIFICIAL INTELLIGENCE'S DANGEROUS RISKS

Although AI has been lauded as revolutionary and game-changing, it is not without flaws.

Elon Musk, the creator of Tesla and SpaceX, offered a friendly warning in March 18 at the South by Southwest tech conference in Austin, Texas: "AI is considerably more hazardous than nukes," he added, billionaire casual in a furry-collared bomber jacket and days' old scruff.

Musk, no shrinking violet when it comes to opining about technology, has repeated a version of these artificial intelligence forewarnings in other contexts as well.

"I am very near... to the cutting edge of AI, and that scares the hell out of me," he told his SXSW audience. "It's capable of much more than practically everyone realizes, and its pace of advancement is exponential."

ARTIFICIAL INTELLIGENCE RISKS

Job loss caused by automation "Deepfakes" violates privacy.

Bad data causes algorithmic bias.

Inequality in society

Volatility in the market

Automatization of weapons

Meanwhile, Musk is far from alone in his pessimistic (some would say bleakly apocalyptic) outlook. A year ago, the late physicist Stephen Hawking warned an audience in Portugal that AI's effects might be deadly unless its rapid advancement is properly and responsibly handled.

"Unless we figure out how to prepare for and minimize the likely threats," he adds, "AI might be the worst event in our civilization's history."

Given the number and size of unfathomably horrible disasters throughout human history, that is quite a feat.

And, just in case we haven't made our argument loud and clear enough, Future of Life Institute researcher Stuart Armstrong has cautioned that if AI goes wild, it will be an "extinction danger." He maintained that nuclear war, he maintained, is on a different level of catastrophe since it would "destroy just a very small portion of the earth." Pandemics, too, "even at their most virulent."

Musk discusses his concerns about artificial intelligence.

"If AI went wrong and murdered 95 percent of humans," he said, "the remaining five percent would be obliterated shortly after." So, despite its vagueness, it has some pretty serious hazards.

How, precisely, may AI reach such a terrible point? Gary Marcus, a cognitive scientist and author, provided some details in a 2013 New Yorker piece. He believes that as robots get smarter, their purposes will change.

"Once computers can easily reprogram and incrementally improve themselves, resulting in a so-called 'technological singularity' or 'intelligence explosion,' the dangers of robots outwitting humans in struggles for resources and self-preservation cannot be disregarded."

ARTIFICIAL INTELLIGENCE A SECURITY RISK

Is Artificial Intelligence a Security Risk?

As AI becomes more powerful and pervasive, the voices warning about its current and prospective dangers will become increasingly audible. Anxiety abounds on a variety of fronts, whether it's the expanding automation of some jobs, gender and racial discrimination worries stemming from outdated information sources or autonomous weapons that operate without human supervision (to name a few). And we are still in the early stages.

Is Artificial Intelligence a Potential Hazard?

The risks posed by artificial intelligence have long been considered in the IT industry. The automation of jobs, the propagation of fake news, and a dangerous arms race with AI-powered weapons have all been cited as serious risks posed by AI.

Destructive superintelligence, defined as artificial general intelligence created by humans and escaping our control to cause havoc, is in a class by itself. It's also something that may or may not become a reality (theory varies), so at this moment it's more of a hypothetical threat—and a constant source of existential dread.

Here are a few examples of how artificial intelligence poses a significant risk:

Job automation is commonly seen as the most pressing issue. The question is no longer whether AI will replace certain types of vocations, but to what extent. Many industries, particularly those where people do predictable and repetitive tasks, are already experiencing upheaval. According to a 2019 Brookings Institution study, 36 million people work in occupations with "high exposure" to automation, implying that at least 70% of their operations—ranging from retail sales and market analysis to hospitality and warehouse labor—will be done using AI within the next few years. A more recent Brookings study implies that white-collar jobs may be under more jeopardy. According to a 2018 McKinsey & Company study, the African American workforce will suffer significantly.

The reason we have a low unemployment number, which doesn't actually represent those who aren't looking for work, is largely because this economy has generated rather substantially lower-wage service sector jobs, "legendary futurist Martin Ford told Built In. "I don't think that will continue."

He added that as AI robots get smarter and more dexterous, the same tasks would require fewer workers. And, while AI will create jobs, an undetermined proportion of which will be open to less educated segments of the of the displaced labor force, many will be unavailable to them.

"Will one of these new vocations be a good fit for you if you're flipping burgers at McDonald's and more automation comes in?" According to Ford. Ford. Or is it possible that the new career will require extensive schooling or training, or perhaps natural talents — exceptional interpersonal skills or ingenuity — that you do not have?" Or is it possible that the new career will require extensive schooling or training, or perhaps natural talents — exceptional interpersonal skills or ingenuity — that you do not have?" Because those are the things that computers, at least so far, are not especially excellent at.

John C. Havens, author of Heartificial Intelligence: Embracing Humanity and Maximizing Machines, believes AI will create as many or more jobs than it will displace.

Havens recalls questioning the CEO of a law firm about machine learning around four years ago. The entrepreneur desired to hire more employees, but he was also under pressure to meet a certain amount of profit for his shareholders. He discovered that a $200,000 piece of software could replace ten people earning $100,000 a year. He'd save $800,000 as a result. The software would also increase productivity by 70% and eliminate around 95% of errors. From a fully shareholder-centric, single bottom-line perspective, Havens From a fully shareholder-centric, single bottom-line perspective, Havens stated that "there is no legal reason why he shouldn't fire all the people." Would he be upset about it? Of course, But that's not the point.

Even positions that need doctorates and more post-college training are vulnerable to AI displacement. According to technology expert Chris Messina, some of them may be wiped. AI is already having a significant impact on medicine. According to Messina, law and accounting are up next, with the former expecting "a tremendous shakeup."

"Think about the complexities of contracts and genuinely going into and understanding what it takes to build a faultless transaction framework," he continued. "Hundreds or thousands of pages of data and papers are being examined by a large number of attorneys. attorneys. attorneys. It's quite simple to overlook anything. So, AI that can comb through and completely give the best possible contract for the outcome you're looking for is likely to replace a lot of corporate attorneys.

Messina cautioned accountants to brace themselves for a major transformation. Once AI is capable of swiftly sifting through massive amounts of data to make autonomous decisions based on computational interpretations, human auditors may become obsolete.

PRIVACY, SECURITY, AND THE EMERGENCE OF "DEEPFAKES "

While job loss is presently the most significant concern associated with AI disruption, it is only one of several possible threats. In a February 2018 paper titled "The Malicious Use of Artificial Intelligence: Forecasting, Prevention, and Mitigation," 26 researchers from 14 institutions (academic, civil, and industrial) listed a slew of other risks that could cause serious harm — or, at the very least, minor chaos — in less than five years.

"Malicious use of AI," they wrote in their 100-page report, "could threaten digital security (e.g., criminals training machines to hack or socially engineer victims at human or superhuman levels of performance), physical security (e.g., non-state actors weaponizing consumer drones), and political security (e.g., privacy-eroding surveillance, profiling, and repression, or automated and targeted disinformation campaigns."

In addition to its more serious concerns, Ford is concerned about how AI may negatively impact privacy and security. He cited China's "Orwellian" usage of facial recognition technology in offices, schools, and other settings as an example. But it is only one country. "A complete ecosphere" of businesses that specialize in the same technology and sell it all over the world.

We can only speculate on whether this technology will ever become commonplace. Could round-the-clock, AI-analysed monitoring ultimately appear asasas an acceptable trade-off for greater safety and security, similar to how we blindly sacrifice our digital data at the altar of convenience on the internet?

"Authoritarian regimes use or will use it," Ford said. "The question is, how far does it infect Western nations and democracies, and what constraints do we impose on it?"

"Authoritarian regimes use or intend to use it... The question is, "How far does it penetrate Western nations and democracies, and what constraints do we impose on it?"

AI will also create hyper-realistic social media "personalities" that are incredibly difficult to distinguish from genuine ones, according to Ford. AI will also create hyper-realistic social media "personalities" that are incredibly difficult to distinguish from genuine ones, according to Ford. AI will also create hyper-realistic social media "personalities" that are incredibly difficult to distinguish from genuine ones, according to Ford. They may have an impact on an election if deployed cheaply and at scale on Twitter, Facebook, or Instagram.

The same is true for so-called audio and video deepfakes, which are created by altering voices and likenesses. The latter is already making waves. Ford, on the other hand, believes that the former will become extremely difficult. Using machine learning, a branch of AI that specializes in natural language processing, an audio clip of any given politician may be altered to appear as though that person uttered racist or sexist sentiments when, in fact, they did not. If the quality of the video is excellent enough to deceive the audience and avoid detection, Ford says it could "totally wreck a political campaign."

And it just takes one success.

"No one knows what's genuine and what's not from then on," he remarked. So it leads to a situation in which you literally cannot trust your own eyes and hearing; you cannot rely on what we have historically considered to be the best possible evidence. . . That is going to be a tremendous problem.

While lawmakers are often not tech-savvy, they are on high alert and seeking answers.

AI BIAS AND WIDENING SOCIOECONOMIC INEQUALITY

Another cause for concern is the widening social imbalance caused by AI-driven job losses. Along with education, labor has always been a driver of social mobility. However, when it comes to a certain type of work— the predictable, repetitive kind that is vulnerable to AI takeover—research takeover research has shown that employees who are out in the cold are far less likely to acquire or seek retraining than those in higher-level positions with more money. (Of course, not everyone believes that.)

AI prejudice of many kinds is also dangerous. Princeton computer science professor Olga Russakovsky recently told the New York Times that it goes far beyond gender and color. Aside from data and algorithmic bias (the latter of which may "amplify" the former), AI is produced by humans, and humans are naturally biased.

"A.I. researchers are often men from certain ethnic groups who grew up in high socioeconomic zones, and they are mostly people without impairments," Russakovsky remarked. "Because we're a pretty homogeneous population, it's difficult to think broadly about foreign concerns."

In the same article, Google researcher Timnit Gebru suggested that bias stems from social rather than technological factors, and she called scientists like herself "some of the most dangerous people in the world, because we have this sense of impartiality." "The scientific profession needs to be located in striving to explain the social dynamics of the world," she noted, "since most of the radical change occurs at the social level."

And engineers aren't the only ones who are concerned about AI's possible socioeconomic ramifications. Along with journalists and politicians, Pope Francis is speaking out—and he isn't only whistling Sanctus. At a late-September Vatican summit titled "The Common Good in the Digital Age," Francis cautioned" Francis cautioned" Francis cautioned that AI had the potential to "poison public discussions and even control the ideas of millions of people, to the point of threatening the very institutions that guarantee peaceful civil coexistence."

"If mankind's so-called technological progress were to become an opponent of the common good," he warned, "this would result in a regretful regression to a form of barbarism enforced by the rule of the strongest."

A big part of the problem, according to Messina, is the private sector's thirst for profit above everything else. Because "that's what they're supposed to do," he explained, as a result, they're not thinking, 'What's the best thing here?' Here?" " What has the best chance of succeeding?"

"The thought is, 'If we can do it, let's try it and see what, 'happens,'" he added. "'And if we can profit from it, we'll do a lot of it.' However, this is not limited to technology. That has always happened.

AUTONOMOUS WEAPONS AND A POTENTIAL AI ARMS RACE

Not everyone, including Ford, agrees with Musk that AI is more dangerous than nuclear weapons. But what if AI decides to use nukes or biological weapons without human intervention? What if an adversary uses data manipulation data manipulation data manipulation to send AI-guided missiles back to where they came from? Both are possibilities. And both would be terrible. More than 30,000 AI/robotics professionals and others who signed an open letter on the subject in 2015 undoubtedly agree.

"The critical option for humanity now is whether to commence or halt a global AI arms race," they said. "If any significant military power pursues AI weapon development, a global arms race is absolutely inescapable, and the aim of this technological trajectory is clear: autonomous weapons will become tomorrow's Kalashnikovs."

Unlike nuclear weapons, they do not require expensive or difficult-to-obtain raw materials, so they will be ubiquitous and economical for all significant military states to mass-produce. It will only be a matter of time until they appear on the black market and end up in the hands of terrorists, rulers seeking to better control their populations, warlords seeking ethnic cleansing, and so on. Autonomous weapons are ideal for assassinations, undermining regimes, subduing populations, and selectively executing certain ethnic groups. As a result, we believe that a military AI arms race would be detrimental to humanity. There are several ways in which artificial intelligence may make battlefields safer for humans, particularly civilians, without producing new weapons for murder.

(The Pentagon's budget for 2020 is $718 billion.) Over $1 billion of the money would go into AI and machine learning for things like logistics, intelligence analysis, and, yes, weapons.

A Vox post proposed a scary potential involving the development of a sophisticated AI system "with the goal of, say, estimating some number with high confidence." confidence." confidence." " The AI knows that using all of the world's computer hardware will give it more confidence in its calculations, and it realizes that using a biological superweapon to wipe out humans will give it unrestricted access to all of the hardware. "After" annihilating humanity, it can more confidently estimate the number."

That is really uncomfortable. But don't worry. The Obama Administration's Department of Defense released a directive on "Autonomy in Weapon Systems" in 2012, which said that "autonomous and semiautonomous weapon systems should be designed to allow commanders and operators to exercise acceptable degrees of human judgment over the use of force."

In early November of this year, the Defense Innovation Board, a Pentagon group, set ethical rules regulating the design and deployment of AI-enabled weapons. However, according to the Washington Post, "the board's recommendations are not legally binding." It is now up to the Pentagon to decide how and whether to continue working with them.

That's great news. Or not.

Have you ever considered that algorithms may bring our whole financial system down? Wall Street, you are correct. You should take notice of this. Algorithmic trading might be to blame for the next major financial calamity in the markets.

What exactly is algorithmic trading? This kind of trading occurs when a computer, free of the impulses or emotions that might cloud a human's judgment, executes trades based on pre-programmed instructions. These computers may conduct very high-volume, high-frequency, and high-value trades, resulting in massive losses and significant market instability. Algorithmic High-Frequency Trading (HFT) has been shown to be a significant risk factor in our markets. HFT is simply when a computer does hundreds of transactions at breakneck rates with the intention of selling them a few seconds later for a small profit. Thousands of these transactions every second might add up to a substantial sum of money. The problem with HFT is that it ignores how interconnected the markets are as well as the reality that human emotion and logic still play a role in our markets.

A sell-off of millions of shares in the airline market may possibly frighten people into selling their shares in the hotel business, which could then snowball into people selling their interests in other travel-related industries, affecting logistics companies, food supply companies, and so on.

As an example, consider the May 2010 "Flash Crash." The Dow Jones plummeted 1,000 points (more than $1 trillion in value) towards the end of the trading day before recovering to normal levels just 36 minutes later. What caused this collision? The disaster was started by a London-based trader named Navinder Singh Sarao, and it was exacerbated by HFT machines. Sarao seems to have used a "spoofing" algorithm to make an order for thousands of stock index futures contracts, betting that the market would crash. Instead of carrying out the wager, Sarao planned to cancel the order at the last minute and buy the lower-priced equities that were being sold off as a result of his first bet. Other individuals and HFT computers perceived this $200 million gamble as a sign that the market was ready to crash. As a result, HFT computers precipitated one of the largest stock sell-offs in history, causing a global loss of more than $1 trillion in a single day.

Financial HFT algorithms are not always correct. We believe that computers are the be-all and end-all of accuracy, yet AI is only as smart as the humans who created it. In 2012, Knight Capital Group was on the verge of bankruptcy due to an issue. Knight's computers improperly dumped hundreds of orders per second onto the NYSE, causing disastrous chaos for the company. In less than 45 minutes, the HFT algorithms completed 4 million trades involving 397 million shares. Because of the volatility caused by this computer error, Knight lost $460 million overnight and had to be purchased by another company. Errors in algorithms clearly have serious consequences for shareholders and the markets, and no one learned this lesson more painfully than Knight.

Artificial Intelligence Risk Mitigation

Many people believe that regulation is the only way to prevent or at least reduce the most malevolent AI from wreaking devastation.

"I am not normally a proponent of regulation and supervision — I feel one should typically err on the side of restricting such things," Musk said at SXSW.

"It must be a public institution with information and then oversight to ensure that everyone is building AI safely." This is quite significant.

Ford agrees, but only on one condition. He suggested that regulation of AI implementation is OK but not of research itself.

"You restrict how AI is utilized," he said, "but you don't stifle progress in basic technology." That, I feel, would be foolish and maybe hazardous. "

"You control how AI is used... but you don't stifle innovation in underlying technology." That, I feel, would be foolish and maybe hazardous. "

Because any country that falls behind in AI development is at a significant disadvantage—militarily, socially, and economically. Ford went on to say that the solution is selective application:

"We decide where we want AI and where we don't; where it's acceptable and where it isn't." And other countries will make other choices. So, China may have it everywhere, but it doesn't mean we can afford to fall behind in terms of technology. "

Speaking at Princeton University on autonomous weapons, American General John R. Allen emphasized the need for "a dynamic international debate that can understand what this technology is." If necessary, he said, there should be a discussion on how best to manage it, whether via a treaty that completely prohibits AI weapons or one that allows just restricted uses of the technology.

Safer AI, according to Havens, starts and ends with humans. His main point, which he elaborates on in his 2016 book, is: "How can robots know what we value if we don't know ourselves?" He noted that while building AI solutions, it is critical to "respect end-user values with a human-centric perspective" rather than focus on short-term profitability.

"Since the dawn of humanity, technology has been capable of assisting humans with labor," Havens wrote in Heartificial Intelligence. However, as a species, we've never faced the genuine possibility that computers may become smarter than humans or be imbued with conscience. This technological milestone is crucial to recognize, both to raise the quest to respect mankind and to clearly convey how AI may improve it. That is why we must be aware of the occupations we wish to teach robots to do in an educated manner. This involved both individual and communal choice.

The World Economic Forum discusses the implementation of ethical AI.

Fei-Fei Li and John Etchemendy of Stanford University's Institute for Human-Centered Artificial Intelligence share this sentiment. In a recent blog post, they urged the combining of diverse experts from various businesses to guarantee that AI realizes its full potential and benefits society rather than harming it.

"Our future depends on the ability of social and computer scientists to collaborate with people from varied backgrounds—a significant shift from today's computer science-centric approach," they said. "AI creators must seek the perspectives, experiences, and concerns of people of all ethnicities, genders, cultures, and socioeconomic groups, as well as those from other fields such as economics, law, medicine, philosophy, history, sociology, communications, human-computer interaction, psychology, and Science and Technology Studies (STS)" (STS). This collaboration should take place throughout the life of an application, from its early phases of development through its market launch and as its usage grows.

Messina is positive about what should happen to help prevent an AI catastrophe, but he is skeptical that it will ever happen. Government regulation, he continued, isn't a given, especially in light of failures in the social media industry, whose technological sophistication pales in comparison to that of AI. It will take a "major effort" on the part of huge tech businesses to limit expansion for the purpose of improved sustainability and fewer unintended impacts—especially catastrophic ones.

"At the present," he said, "I don't feel the onus is on it to happen."

According to Messina, getting to that point will require some kind of "catalyst." A catastrophic trigger, such as war or economic collapse, However, whether such an event would be "large enough to really affect significant long-term change is debatable."

Ford, for one, remains a long-term optimist despite being "quite un-bullish" on AI.

"I think we can discuss all of these worries, and they are very serious, but AI will also be the most powerful weapon in our armoury for addressing the most pressing challenges we have," including climate change.

His concerns about the near future, on the other hand, are more intense.

We need to be smarter," he said. "I am concerned about these challenges and our ability to adjust to them over the next decade or two."

CHAPTER FOUR

THE AGE OF DATA SCIENCE

Data science is the process of extracting valuable insights from raw data. This book will walk you through the fundamentals of data science, including how it works and examples of how it is used today.

What Exactly Is Data Science?

Simply put, data science is dedicated to extracting clean information from raw data in order to provide meaningful insights.

And there is a wealth of information available. It is estimated that by 2025, there will be around 175 zettabytes of data floating around (a zettabyte is a trillion gigabytes) (a zettabyte is a trillion gigabytes). Data has been dubbed the "oil of the twenty-first century." So, what are we going to do with all of this information? How can we make it work for us? What are its practical applications? These are data science-related questions.

What exactly is data science?

Data science is the process of extracting useful information from huge volumes of noisy data using tools and procedures. Data science is used for everything from business decision making to sports analytics to assessing insurance risk.

The field of data science is rapidly evolving and changing numerous industries. It has enormous benefits in business, research, and our everyday lives. Your commute to work, your most recent search engine query for the nearest coffee shop, your Instagram post about what you ate, and even your fitness tracker's health data are all relevant to different data scientists in different ways. Data science is responsible for providing new commodities, creating breakthrough insights, and making our lives more pleasant by sifting through massive data lakes in search of connections and patterns.

What Exactly Is a Data Scientist?

Someone who specializes in the process of acquiring, organizing, and analyzing data in order to communicate the information as a coherent story with actionable insights. In general, data scientists are skilled in detecting patterns hidden within massive volumes of data, and they often apply complicated algorithms and machine learning models to aid businesses and organizations in making accurate assessments and projections. The typical data scientist is well-versed in math and statistics, as well as computer languages such as R, Python, and SQL.

What Is the Role of a Data Scientist?

What Is the Process of Data Science?

Data science combines several disciplines to provide a complete, thorough, and polished perspective on raw data. While some data scientists specialize in specific areas of the field, others are generalists with skills in data engineering, math, statistics, advanced computing, and visualization, and are able to effectively sift through muddled masses of information and communicate only the most important bits that will help drive innovation and efficiency.

To construct models and make predictions using algorithms and other methodologies, data scientists usually rely heavily on artificial intelligence, especially its subfields of machine learning and deep learning.

Data science may be conceived of as having five stages:

Data collection, data input, signal reception, and data extraction are all examples of capture.

Data warehousing, data cleansing, data staging, data processing, and data architecture must all be maintained.

Data mining, clustering and classification, data modeling, and data summarization are all part of the process.

Data analysis includes data reporting, data visualization, business intelligence, and decision making.

Communicate—exploratory and confirmatory analysis, predictive analysis, regression, text mining, and qualitative analysis are all examples of communication.

Roles Of Data Science And Understanding

Data scientists collect, analyze, and visualize data and, on occasion, create machine learning algorithms.

A data analyst is in charge of obtaining, cleaning, analyzing, and reporting data, as well as sometimes monitoring web analytics.

Data is used by business analysts to provide actionable business insights for the rest of the company.

Data engineers design, build, and manage data pipelines that serve as test environments for data scientists to run algorithms.

Machine learning engineers design and build machine learning systems.

Data Science Understanding

There is no one answer to the question, "What does a data scientist do?" As a result, the particular competencies and toolboxes required by data science practitioners vary by job.

However, there are certain general skills to develop that can help aspiring and early-career data science workers succeed. These include abilities in:

Programming entails using programming languages such as Python and R.

Database administration is the study and use of SQL to interface with databases.

Statistics entails understanding how to evaluate data in order to solve problems.

Furthermore, competent data scientists usually have a few essential soft skills, such as:

Curiosity: the desire to solve problems and discover new things.

Storytelling is the ability to tell stories using data and share insights.

Communication: the ability to interact with others and effectively explain problems and solutions.

Of course, data scientists will need to acquire additional skills and approaches if they want to pursue more specific fields within data science, such as deep learning, neural networks, and natural language processing.

Applications in Data Science

Data science enables us to achieve critical goals that were previously unattainable or required much more time and effort, such as:

Data Science: Examples and Applications

Detecting anomalies (fraud, illness, and criminality) (fraud, disease, and crime)

classification (background checks; an email server recognizing "important" correspondence)

Sales, revenue, and client retention forecasting (sales, revenue, and customer retention)

Detection of patterns (weather patterns, financial market trends) (weather patterns, financial market trends)

Facial, voice, and text recognition (facial, voice, and text)

Recommendations (recommendation systems may steer you to movies, restaurants, and literature based on your learned tastes) (Based on learned preferences, recommendation engines can refer you to movies, restaurants, and books.)

Regression (predicting property values based on characteristics, calculating food delivery times) (predicting food delivery times, predicting home prices based on amenities)

Scheduling ride-share pickups and package deliveries (scheduling ride-share pickups and package deliveries)

Here are a few more detailed examples of how businesses use data science to innovate and disrupt their industries, create new products, and make the environment around them more efficient:

Data Science in Healthcare

Data science has resulted in a number of accomplishments in the healthcare industry. With a massive network of data now available through everything from EMRs to clinical databases to personal activity trackers, medical practitioners are experimenting with new methods to study illness, practice preventative care, diagnose diseases more quickly, and investigate novel treatment options. Because patient data is so sensitive, data security is a major problem in the healthcare industry.

Self-Driving Car Data Science

Data science is also on the horizon. Tesla, Ford, and Volkswagen have all included predictive analytics in their self-driving vehicles. These vehicles use hundreds of miniature cameras and sensors to transmit data in real time. Self-driving cars may adapt to speed limits, avoid risky lane changes, and even take passengers on the shortest route by using machine learning, predictive analytics, and data science.

Logistics and data science.

UPS has pledged to use data science to improve efficiency both internally and along its delivery routes. ORION (On-road Integrated Optimization and Navigation) technology from the firm uses data science-backed statistical modeling and algorithms to determine optimal routes for delivery trucks based on weather, traffic, and construction. Data science is expected to save the logistics sector millions of gallons of fuel and delivery miles every year.

Data Science in the Entertainment Industry

Do you ever wonder how Spotify seems to recommend the perfect song for you? Or how does Netflix know just which shows you'll like binge-watching? These media streaming behemoths use data science to analyze your preferences and select content from their massive libraries that they believe will adequately appeal to your interests.

Data Science in Product, Sales, and Marketing

Many businesses rely on data scientists to build time-series forecasting models that help with inventory management and supply chain optimization. Data scientists are sometimes tasked with developing proactive recommendations based on budget predictions generated by financial models. Some even use data mining to segment customers depending on their behavior, tailoring future marketing messages to specific groups based on previous brand encounters.

Finance Data Science

Machine learning and data analytics have saved the banking industry millions of dollars and incalculable hours. JP Morgan's contract intelligence platform, for example, analyzes and extracts critical data from thousands of commercial credit agreements each year using natural language processing. What would have taken hundreds of thousands of labor hours to complete is now completed in a matter of hours thanks to data science. Furthermore, fintech companies like Stripe and PayPal invest in data science to build machine learning algorithms that detect and prevent fraudulent behavior.

Cybersecurity Data Science: Data science is useful in many industries, but it may be especially important in cybersecurity. For example, the global cybersecurity company Kaspersky uses science and machine learning to discover hundreds of thousands of new pieces of malware every day. The ability to swiftly detect and comprehend emerging cybercrime strategies utilizing data science is critical to our future safety and security.

The Internet and its history

The Internet has evolved to revolutionize global communications.

Birth web Science Computing

The Internet has evolved to revolutionize global communications.

Birth to Web Science Computing Web History in Brief A brief history of the Internet

THE WEB AND ITS

JOURNEY

The Internet has evolved to revolutionize global communications.

The birthplace of the World Wide Web

While working at CERN, British scientist Tim Berners-Lee created the World Wide Web (WWW). The Web was created to fulfill the demand for automated information exchange among scientists at colleges and institutions throughout the world.

CERN is not a solitary laboratory, but rather the hub of an international community of approximately 17 000 scientists from over 100 nations. Although they often visit CERN, the scientists mostly work in universities and national laboratories in their own countries. As a result, dependable communication systems are essential. The WWW's major purpose was to integrate the rapidly evolving technologies of computers, data networks, and hypertext into a powerful and easy-to-use worldwide information system.

How the Internet came to be

Tim Berners-Lee created the first World Wide Web proposal in March 1989, followed by a second proposal in May 1990. In November 1990, this was defined as a management plan by Belgian systems expert Robert Cailliau. This described the fundamental ideas as well as key terms underpinning the Web. The article proposed a "hypertext project" called "WorldWideWeb," in which a "web" of "hypertext documents" could be accessed using "browsers." Tim Berners-Lee got the first Web server and browser up and running at CERN by the end of 1990, demonstrating his principles. On a NeXT computer, he built the code for his Web server. To prevent it from being turned off accidentally, the computer had a handwritten note in red ink that read: "This machine is a server. The address sinfo.cern.ch was the address of the world's first website and Web server, which were hosted on a NeXT computer at CERN.

web,Hypertext,Computer,

The WWW design enabled easy access to existing content, and an early web page linked to information useful to CERN scientists (for example, the CERN phone directory and instructions to CERN's core computers). There were no search engines in the early years, so the search function was based on terms. Early Lee's Web browser, which ran on NeXT machines, demonstrated his vision and included many of the features found in modern Web browsers. It also included the first Web editing capability, the ability to modify pages directly from within the browser.

The Web stretches

Only a few people had access to the NeXT computer platform on which the initial browser operated, but work quickly commenced on a simpler, 'line-mode' browser, which could run on any system. It was written by Nicola Pellow during her undergraduate work placement at CERN. In 1991, Berners-Lee launched his WWW program. It contained the 'line-mode' browser, Web server software, and a library for developers. In March 1991, the program became accessible to coworkers using CERN computers. A few months later, in August 1991, he introduced the WWW software on Internet newsgroups, sparking worldwide interest in the project.

Global expansion

The first Web server in the United States went online in December 1991, thanks to the efforts of Paul Kunz and Louise Addis, once again at a particle physics laboratory: the Stanford Linear Accelerator Center (SLAC) in California. There were essentially just two kinds of browsers at the time. The first was the early development version, which was complicated but only available on NeXT machines. The alternative option was the 'line-mode' browser, which was easy to install and use on any platform but limited in capability and use. The small team at CERN was clearly incapable of completing all of the work necessary to further improve the system, so Berners-Lee issued an open call on the internet for new developers to join in. Several people worked on browsers, mostly for the X-Window System. MIDAS by Tony Johnson of SLAC, Viola by Pei Wei of technical publisher O'Reilly Books, and Erwise by Finnish students from Helsinki University of Technology were among them. The National Center for Supercomputing Applications (NCSA) at the University of Illinois released the initial version of its Mosaic browser in early 1993. This software ran under the popular X Window System environment, which allowed for pleasant window-based interaction. Shortly afterward, the NCSA released versions for the PC and Macintosh platforms. The availability of dependable, user-friendly browsers on these popular PCs had an immediate influence on the WWW's expansion. At the end of the same year, the European Commission authorized its first web project (WISE), with CERN as one of the partners. On April 30, 1993, CERN declared the WorldWideWeb source code royalty-free, thereby declaring it free software. By late 1993, there were over 500 known web servers, and the

WWW accounted for 1% of internet traffic (the rest being remote access, e-mail, and file transfer). The year 1994 was dubbed "The Year of the Web." The first International World Wide Web Conference, organized by Robert Cailliau, was held in May at CERN. It drew 380 users and developers and was dubbed the "Woodstock of the Web." As 1994 progressed, news of the Web filled the media. In October, the NCSA and the newly created International WWW Conference Committee (IW3C2) sponsored a second conference in the United States, which was attended by 1300 individuals (IW3C2). The Web had 10,000 servers, 2000 of which were commercial, and 10 million users by the end of 1994. Traffic was similar to transmitting Shakespeare's full collected works each second. The technology was continuously updated to meet new needs. The two most major upgrades that were soon to be incorporated were security and e-commerce features.

Standards that are open

One important point was that the web should remain an open standard for everyone to use, and that no one should lock it up in a proprietary system. In this spirit, CERN proposed "WebCore" to the European Union Commission under the ESPRIT initiative. The initiative's goal was to create a global consortium in collaboration with the Massachusetts Institute of Technology (MIT) in the United States (MIT). Berners-Lee left CERN in 1994 to join MIT and form the International World Wide Web Consortium (W3C) (W3C). Meanwhile, with the LHC project nearing completion, CERN thought that extra web development was a distraction from the laboratory's main purpose. W3C was looking for a new European partner. The European Commission delegated CERN's tasks to the French National Institute for Research in Computer Science and Controls (INRIA). In April 1995, INRIA became the first European W3C host in April, followed by Keio University of Japan (Shonan Fujisawa Campus) in Asia in 1996. In 2003, INRIA relinquished the status of European W3C Host to ERCIM (European Research Consortium in Informatics and Mathematics). Beihang University was appointed the fourth host by W3C in 2013.

He is the co-founder of Global Optimism, co-host of the podcast "Outrage & Optimism," and co-author of the recently published book "The Future We Choose: Surviving the Climate Crisis."

Rivett-Carnac is a Global Optimism founding partner and co-author of The Future We Choose.

Before COVID-19 blasted into our world, governments had to deal with two major issues: the drop in oil prices and the climate crisis. Now that three crises have intertwined, the way through them may as well be with billions of dollars in stimulus, we can rebuild clean and healthy, shifting away from fossil fuels to clean infrastructure and businesses that create millions of jobs, address fundamental social inequities, and develop a dynamic economy.

In our book, "We Owe The Future" We Choose, we explain two possible futures: one in which we act to cut emissions in half by the end of this decade, and the one envisioned in the extract below if we fail.

It is 2050. Aside from the emissions reductions achieved in 2015, no new efforts to restrict emissions were made. We are on track to have a globe that is more than 3 degrees warmer by 2100.

The air is the first thing that touches you.

Many parts of the world have hot, dense air that is polluted with particles depending on the time of day. Your eyes regularly get wet. Your cough doesn't seem to go away. You can't simply go out your front door and breathe fresh air. Instead, you check your phone before opening doors or windows in the morning to see what the air quality will be. Everything seems to be in order—

sunny and clear—but you know otherwise. When storms and heat waves overlap and cluster, the resulting air pollution and elevated surface ozone levels may make it dangerous to go outside without a properly designed face mask (which few can afford) or a properly designed face mask (which only some can afford).

Our planet is becoming hotter, an irreversible occurrence that is now completely beyond our control. We've already passed critical junctures, such as the Great Melting of the Arctic Sea ice, which used to block the sun's heat. Oceans, forests, plants, trees, and soil have long absorbed half of the carbon dioxide we emit. There are few residual trees, most of which have been cut or destroyed by wildfire, and the permafrost is releasing greenhouse gases into an already overburdened atmosphere.

Massive sections of the planet will become inhospitable to humans within the next five to ten years. We don't know how habitable Australia, North Africa, and western North America will be by 2100. Nobody knows what the future will bring for their children and grandchildren.

More moisture in the atmosphere and warmer sea surface temperatures have resulted in an increase in strong hurricanes and tropical storms. Coastal cities in

Bangladesh, Mexico, the United States, and others have suffered massive infrastructure destruction and flooding, killing thousands and displacing millions. This has become more common recently.

Because many disasters often occur at the same time, it may take weeks or even months for critical food and water supplies to reach areas ravaged by severe floods. Malaria, dengue fever, cholera, respiratory illnesses, and malnutrition are all widespread.

Melting permafrost is exposing ancient microbes to which modern humans have never been exposed and, as a result, have no defense. Mosquito and tick-borne diseases are frequent as these species thrive in the changing environment, spreading to previously safe corners of the globe and gradually overpowering mankind. Worse, as the population has become denser in habitable areas and temperatures have risen, the public health crisis of antibiotic resistance has only worsened.

Every day, because of rising sea levels, some people must migrate to higher ground. Every day, you see photos of mothers hiking through flood waters with their babies strapped on their backs. According to news reports, people are living in houses with water up to their ankles because they have nowhere else to go, their children are ill and wheezing due to mildew developing in their beds, and insurance companies have declared bankruptcy, leaving survivors with no way to rebuild their lives.

Those who remain on the beach must now see the end of a fishing-dependent way of life. As the oceans absorbed carbon dioxide, the water became more acidic, and it is now so harmful to marine life that all but a few countries have banned fishing, even in international waters. Many people argue that the few remaining fish should be enjoyed while they last, an argument that is hard to refute in many parts of the world since it applies to so much that is vanishing.

As disastrous as rising sea levels have been, inland droughts and heat waves have created a unique hell. Vast regions have experienced significant aridification, which is sometimes followed by desertification. There is no longer any wildlife there.

Cities like Marrakech and Volgograd are on the verge of turning into deserts. For years, Hong Kong, Barcelona, Abu Dhabi, and other cities have been desalinating seawater in order to keep up with the continual influx of immigrants from locations that have become dry.

Extreme heat is on the way. Summer temperatures in Paris often reach 111°F (43.8°C). This is no longer a newsworthy occurrence as it would have been 30 years ago. Everyone stays inside, drinks water, and fantasizes about air conditioning. You lie on your couch with a cold, wet towel over your face, attempting to unwind without thinking about the destitute farmers on the outskirts of town who, despite periodic droughts and wildfires, are still trying to plant grapes, olives, or soy—luxuries for the wealthy, not you.

You try not to think about the 2 billion people who live in the hottest areas of the planet, where temperatures may reach 140°F (60°C) for up to 45 days each year — a threshold at which the human body cannot stay outdoors for more than six hours because it loses its capacity to cool itself down. For example, it is becoming more difficult to live there. People tried to stay for a while, but when you can't work outside, when you can only sleep for a couple of hours at 4 a.m. because that's the coolest time of day, there's not much you can do except go. Mass migrations to less hot rural areas are plagued by a slew of refugee concerns, societal unrest, and violence over diminishing water resources.

Even in some parts of the United States, there are heated battles over water between the wealthy, who are willing to pay for as much water as they want, and everyone else who wants fair access to the life-giving resource. Almost all public restroom faucets are guarded, and those in restrooms are coin-operated. At the federal level, Congress is in a frenzy about water redistribution: states with less water demand their fair share from those with more. For years, government officials have been unable to reach an agreement, and the Colorado River and the Rio Grande continue to dwindle.

Depending on where you live, food production fluctuates greatly from month to month and season to season. There are more hungry people than ever before. Because climate zones have shifted, some new agricultural areas have emerged (Alaska, the Arctic), while others have dried up (Mexico, California). Others are in danger owing to the extreme heat, not to mention floods, wildfires, and storms.

But one thing is constant: if you have money, you have access. Global trade has slowed as countries such as China stop exporting and try to hold on to their own resources. Disasters and wars wreak havoc on trade routes. The tyranny of supply and demand is becoming more severe; as food becomes scarcer, it may become absurdly expensive. Income inequality has never been more visible or dangerous.

Governments are as committed to keeping money and resources inside their borders as they are to keeping people out. The militaries of the majority of nations are today just extremely militarized border patrols. Lockdown is the goal, although it hasn't been entirely successful. Desperate individuals will always find a way.

Since the equatorial belt became uninhabitable, a steady tide of migrants has been pouring north from Central America into Mexico and the United States. Others are moving south, toward the southernmost points of Chile and Argentina. The same situations are being played out in Europe and Asia. Some countries have been more global Good Samaritans than others, but even those have now effectively closed their doors, wallets, and eyes.

Even if you live in a more temperate climate, such as Canada or Scandinavia, you are still vulnerable. Severe tornadoes, flash floods, wildfires, mudslides, and blizzards are all possibilities. You may have a fully stocked storm cellar, an emergency go-bag in your car, or a six-foot fire moat encircling your house, depending on where you reside. People are obsessed with weather forecasts. Only the most daring turn their phones off at night. If an emergency occurs, you may only have a few minutes to respond.

The weather is unavoidable, but recent news about what's going on at the borders has been too much for most people to bear. Under rising criticism from public health specialists, news organizations have reduced the number of pieces on genocide, slavery, and refugee virus outbreaks. The news can no longer be trusted. Social media, long a depressing source of live feeds and disaster reporting, is now overrun by conspiracy theories and doctored footage.

The destiny of the human species is increasingly being contested. For many, the only uncertainty is how long we will live and how many generations will come after us. Suicides are the most visible manifestation of the widespread despair, but there are other signs as well: unfathomable loss, unbearable guilt, and profound resentment of previous generations for failing to do what was necessary to avert this unavoidable disaster.

CHAPTER FIVE

THE FUTURE WE CHOOSE

IS BEYOND MEASURE

Adapted from THE FUTURE WE CHOOSE: How to Survive the Climate Crisis. The Bajau people dwell on the sea along Malaysia's coast. Bajau fishermen are reported to free dive more than 20 meters into the water in search of seafood. Because children spend so much time in the ocean when their eyes are developing, they have exceptional underwater vision. Their ocular muscles have grown to constrict the pupils even more and to change the shape of the lens to enhance light refraction.

A typical Zimbabwean cottage

Zimbabwe's traditional village home. Western civilization is a "carpentered world." Certain African tribes, on the other hand, who often live-in round huts with round entrances, can not perceive straight lines or perspective as vividly as those who live in square structures. Mark Foster: Photographer

We humans inherited a lot, but the most important thing we received was the ability to transcend our ancestors.

We may be able to rethink what it means to be human today thanks to advances in science and technology—research in animal and ape behavior on the one hand, and psychology and neuroscience on the other. We humans inherited a lot, but the most important thing we received was the ability to transcend our ancestors. This is what we've done the whole trip. We may look to our history, from our origins in Africa to our global expansion, and to the bands, tribes, city-states, and civilizations we built throughout our time on Earth. We may examine the origins, history, and justification of our institutions, including religious, political, economic, ecological, educational, and humanitarian organizations.

We are confronted with a reality that is vastly different from that of our forefathers. But we can understand and handle today's difficulties, many of which are man-made, if we first understand who we are and how the past has created us. We must understand what is constant in our nature and recognize what we can and must intentionally change in order to participate in our own advancement.

Our human adventure began more than 300,000 years ago, and understanding it will lead us to the next step. One that is unmistakably human.

Our human adventure began more than 300,000 years ago, and understanding it will lead us to the next step. One that is unmistakably human.

Emerging technologies and the risks of global disaster

For the first time, the industrial scale development of nuclear weapons in the 1950s meant that, for the first time, a few world leaders had the ability to slaughter hundreds of millions of people. This was a dramatic turning point in a long-term trend: as technology advances and the global economy grows, it becomes easier to wreak havoc on a larger and larger scale.

We expect this trend to continue in the twenty-first century. New transformative technologies may promise a substantially improved future, but they also pose catastrophic risks. Mitigating these concerns while increasing the possibility that these technologies will allow future generations to flourish may be the century's most pressing problem.

A growing movement is attempting to address these challenges, with new research institutes opening at

Cambridge, MIT, and Oxford. Nonetheless, work on reducing multiple risks is tragically ignored, with just a few scholars paying attention in certain cases. We feel that discovering an effective way to work on these difficulties may be the most beneficial thing you can do.

Developing the capacity to research and solve problems

Comparing global concerns involves a lot of uncertainty and difficult judgment calls, and there have been surprisingly few serious attempts to make such broad picture parallels. And there are countless global issues that have yet to be adequately addressed.

For these reasons, we strongly favor work that might help remove some of this uncertainty, as well as work that seems to be significantly useful on many different assumptions, yielding varying conclusions about what to concentrate on.

One key goal in this field is to establish a new discipline of "global priorities" research in order to determine which global challenges are most pressing and to make progress on fundamental questions about how to effectively address them.

Another approach is to help large existing institutions increase their ability to make tough decisions and so deal with global challenges.

A third alternative is to create communities of people who want to do good in an effective way, with the assumption that they will be able to deal with future difficulties as they arise. We're especially thrilled to grow the effective altruism group, as it obviously wants to work on whatever global challenges will be most important in the future. We consider ourselves to be members of this group since we share this goal.

Finally, we want to encourage people to look into issues where the justification for impact is more speculative but potentially critical, such as boosting civilizational resilience, limiting great power conflict, or laying the groundwork for space administration. Making progress on these less explored difficulties (especially from a longtermist standpoint) may help establish and develop these budding fields, or it may help us understand why they're less promising, allowing others to work more effectively and efficiently.

Particularly pressing global issues (our current overall list)

If we had to rank the problem areas, we've investigated so far in terms of the overall effectiveness of additional work on them (assuming the same degree of personal fit for each), our ranking would be as follows.

It should be noted that this is not a rating of which global issues we feel are the most important overall, but rather a ranking of which problems we believe are the most urgent for people who usually share our beliefs and may follow our advice to work on right now.

For this reason, we believe that this list will evolve to some extent from year to year (perhaps with the addition or reduction of one or two worries every year) when conditions change, such as when current problems become less neglected or new ones emerge.

Areas of highest importance

Influencing the progress of artificial intelligence in a positive way

Global research priorities

Developing Effective Altruism

Reducing global catastrophic biological threats

There are more global concerns that we haven't looked at as thoroughly but which seem to be just as critical as the ones listed above. We'd love to see a sizable minority of readers research these topics to learn more about them, especially if they have an exceptionally strong fit for working on them. As an example.

Mitigating big power clashes

Global administration n

Space administration

Check out the rest of our list of potential high-priority issues.

There may be more worries we haven't considered, or maybe one issue that stands out above all the others in terms of how vital it is to work on-we call this "cause X," and it serves as another reason to do extra research.

Regions with the second-highest importance

These are global concerns that we believe are among the most urgent for more people to work on, but we believe that an additional person working on them will have much less impact than work on our highest priority, all else being equal. Nonetheless, depending on the circumstances, they may easily be someone's first choice.

Nuclear safety

Improving Decision-Making in Institutions

Climate change (major dangers) (extreme risks)

All of the aforementioned categories combine to form what we call our priority problem areas or priority issues.

Other major global issues we've investigated

We'd want to see more individuals working on these issues, but given our broad perspective, they seem to be less essential than our top priorities:

Farming in a factory

International health

You may also discover global concerns that we haven't looked into but that seem important to us (albeit perhaps less urgent than our priority problem areas) listed below.

Do you want to help solve any of these issues?

There are many global challenges that we have not yet thoroughly examined but which, with more investigation, may turn out to be highly promising for people to work on. Below are some of the issues we've looked into briefly.

We'd want to see more of our readers gain expertise and try out projects in these areas than they already do, especially in the first group of themes listed below. This is because we feel it will be instantly advantageous (especially for those who have an extraordinarily strong personal fit for one of these areas or have access to an unusually good opportunity) and because it will allow us to uncover new, highly critical issues.

For these reasons, we believe it makes sense for a significant portion of our readers (say, 10-20%) to investigate new issues such as those outlined below rather than focus on our current priority problem areas. This would be the 10–20% of people who are normally most suited to these disciplines, which usually suggests those who have a pre-existing interest. This is explained further down.

We currently know very few people (who share our priorities) who are working on these areas, so if you have to choose between one of the issues below and one of our highest-priority issues, and you have equally good opportunities and fit for both, we believe working on one of these less explored but potentially very pressing issues is your best bet.

We compiled this list by polling seven consultants and combining their suggestions with our own. We've included several intriguing sites with discussions about the importance of each issue as resources for further reading, although we don't always agree with what these sources say.

It should be noted that the issues in each list are not necessarily in any particular order, and that there may be some overlap between them.

Potential top priorities

The following are some subjects that look to be particularly critical in terms of improving the long-term future. We feel they have the potential to be as important for people to work on as our top priorities, but we haven't researched them well enough to know.

The confrontation of great powers

Global administration

Election reform

Artificial intelligence

Space administration

Improving an individual's intellect or thinking

The global public good

Surveillance

Manufacturing with atomic precision

Promoting positive values in general

The Resilience of Civilization

'S-risks'

Emulation of the whole brain

The Dangers of Stable Totalitarianism

Dangers posed by malicious actors

Protecting liberal democracy

We may need to invest more now in order to spend enough later on future issues.

We'd want to see more discussion and study on many of these themes in the interest of improving the long-term future, and we'd like to help foster such inquiry in the future.

Do you want to work on one of these issues?

If you want to pursue a career centered on any of the obstacles described so far, we can assist you in evaluating your options, making relationships with others who are dealing with similar issues, and maybe even locating job or financial opportunities.

Other long-termist issues

We are also interested in the following issues, but feel that work on them will be significantly less effective in terms of genuinely improving the long-term future than work on the topics stated above.

Economic expansion

Infrastructure and science policy

Harmful migration restrictions

Ageing

Enhancing Institutions to Promote Development

Terraforming and space colonization

Technology for detecting deception

Animal welfare in the wild

Preventing the propagation of misleading ideas on social media

Other global concerns

We feel that the following issues are critical in the near and medium term, and that action on them might be as effective as further effort aimed at reducing animal suffering in factory farming or increasing global health.

However, we do not regard them as highly as those indicated above since they seem to be somewhat less ignored, and action on them is less likely to have a significant impact on the very long-range future.

Mental well-being

Biomedical research and other fundamental sciences.

Improving access to pain relief in disadvantaged countries

Other dangers posed by climate change

Smoking in the poor world

Other issues we've looked at that seem to be less vital to focus on than global health

Which issue should you focus on?

Identifying which issues are most important to you

We made our best guesses above on which global issues should be prioritized by more individuals. You may disagree, or you may desire to do further research before reaching any conclusions.

Taking into account your personal fit

We/I urge our readers to consider how important an issue area is in general, as well as their personal fit for the area—how effective they are likely to be in comparison to the average individual working on the problem, based on their talents and experience. You might conceive of your expected long-term impact in an area as a function of how severe the problem is that you're working on and how much you, in particular, will be able to contribute to resolving it.

The benefits of spreading out among several issues

We do not feel that all of our readers (much less everyone) should work on the topics we have prioritized. Even if our readers all agreed on the general importance of the themes, differences in personal fit would imply that they should be should be spread out among varied problem areas.

Furthermore, as we get more readers, there will be more reasons for them to spread out. The following are two of the most major causes:

As more people work on a subject, the benefits of increased effort diminish. This indicates that a huge number of individuals relative to a problem's ability to absorb people will begin to run out of beneficial chances to make progress on that issue, making it preferable for them to be spread out into other areas.

We want to assist a majority of those who follow our recommendations in pursuing one of the highest-priority issue areas indicated above, but we'd also like to see a large percentage pursue chances in the second and third categories. We want to assist a majority of those who follow our recommendations in pursuing one of the highest-priority issue areas indicated above, but we'd also like to see a large percentage pursue chances in the second and third categories. As previously said, we feel that some of our readers—maybe 10–20readers—maybe 10–20%—will—will have the greatest effect by working on other global issues, especially those we consider to be potentially as important as our top priority subjects.

We think that the justifications for spreading for spreading out across varied problem areas also apply to those wanting to do good using an "effective an "effective altruism" strategy—arguably" strategy—arguably even more so. For example, if the effective altruism organization becomes associated with a certain issue, it may lose its ability to evolve and adapt in the future, which is an additional motivator for people who use this strategy to work on a variety of problem areas.

All of that said, we feel our highest-priority issues are currently underserved in comparison to how important they are, even within the effective altruism community, and we want to continue to focus the majority of our efforts on them for the time being.

BIGGEST PROBLEMS FACING THE U.S. TODAY

The major problems facing the United States today

I recently went out to dinner with a friend, and the conversation turned to politics.

"Racism is the single most serious problem affecting America now," she said.

I acknowledged that racism is an issue, but I argued that it is far from the most serious.

What are the five most pressing issues affecting the United States right States right now, in your opinion? Problems are risks to the well-being of Americans, not just issues or worries.

1. Terrorism

This is my most terrifying worry. I'm not talking about internal terrorism here, but rather international terrorism. Although President Joe Biden's administration tells us that domestic terrorists, particularly parents who protest noisily at school board meetings, pose the greatest threat, I disagree.

Following our withdrawal from Afghanistan, the country has become a safe haven for al-Qaida, ISIS, and other extremist Muslim organizations with a long-term intention of targeting of targeting the United States. Similar jihadist organizations may be found across the Middle East and beyond. While we have been lucky not to have another 9/11, it is quite easy to wreak havoc by destroying a portion of the New York City subway, bridge, or tunnel system, our electronic grid, the Capitol Building, and other critical infrastructure.

2. Armageddon.

Although very unlikely, this is the most likely apocalyptic threat. The nine members of the "nuclear club" are the United States, Russia, China, the United Kingdom, France, India, Pakistan, North Korea, and Israel. The United States and Russia control 90% of the world's nuclear arsenal, which consists of around 14,000 nuclear weapons. Israel has not formally claimed membership in the group, although it is said to have between 75 and 400 warheads. Worryingly, China is reported to have 350 warheads while North Korea has 30 to 40, with the ability to strike the US expanding.

There is still widespread concern about a nuclear-armed Pakistan with ties to terrorist groups in neighboring Afghanistan. Take note of the recent death of its top nuclear scientist, A.Q. Khan, who is said to have considered selling nuclear technology to al-Qaida and to have transferred the knowledge to North Korea.

There is also anxiety about North Korea's weak leadership, as well as a probable escalation of US-China confrontations over Taiwan.

3. COVID and other pandemics

In the wake of Ebola and other pandemics in the United States, almost 700,000 people have died as a result of COVID. The number of illnesses, hospitalizations, and fatalities is now dropping nationwide, owing mostly to immunizations, while tens of thousands of Americans still become sick every day.

According to the CDC, 81% of individuals in the United States and 95% of those aged 65 and over have gotten at least one dose of the COVID-19 vaccination. However, according to a recent Israeli study, the effectiveness of the Pfizer vaccine diminishes after six months, prompting boosters. Even if immunizations reduce the severity of the illness, there is concern about the continuous spread of one variation after another, as well as the possibility of additional pandemics. It is unclear when our economy and life in general will return to "normal" amid masks and lockdowns.

4. Border protection:

Our Border protection, southern border is completely disintegrating, with over 100,000 individuals attempting to enter the country each month. Last year, over 1.6 million arrests were recorded at the border, the most on record (CNN, Oct. 22). CNN, October 22.

Although immigration benefits the United States in many ways, this illegal invasion is a tragedy that weakens our sovereignty and makes a mockery of the rule of law. It is estimated that there are more than 10 million illegal aliens (undocumented noncitizens or whatever you want to call them) in the United States, with many of them taking advantage of our welfare system courtesy of American taxpayers.

Recently, tens of thousands of Haitian migrants flooded the border with Mexico, overwhelming border control border control officers' capacity to jail them and process their asylum requests. Another 20,000 Haitians are reportedly gathering in Central America, ready to cross into the United States. They are abandoning Haiti mostly because of a lack of economic opportunities. As much as one sympathizes, economic misery has never been a viable basis for seeking asylum.

The final fact is that the United States cannot enable whole nations to flee to our shores due to economic difficulties. The United Nations has designated roughly 50 countries as "least developed," with billions of poor people potentially entitled to visit the United States. Our nation's existence and identity could not possibly support this.

5. The inefficiency of our political system

If our political institutions were better at governing, we might be able to deal with all of the issues listed above more effectively. However, it is undeniable that our political system, especially at the federal level, is severely dysfunctional. The two major political parties are incapable of working together to pass necessary legislation and build sound public policy.

Although it is tempting to blame this on the rising polarization of the American people and our coarse political culture, public opinion surveys show that a majority of Americans favor moderate viewpoints on most issues, including abortion, gay rights, immigration, law enforcement, and others. Leadership that reflects majority feelings but has yet to be organized is required.

On one hand, we have the Republican Party, which is still trying to recover from Donald Trump's shaky government. On the other hand, we have a Biden administration that claimed to unite the nation and rule from the center but has succumbed to the Democratic Party's extreme left in pursuing a radical social welfare state agenda closer to socialist Bernie Sanders and a woke agenda loyal to "the Squad."

Other issues to consider are climate change, crime, healthcare expenditures, drug addiction, education, and, yes, racism. However, they are not at the top of my list.

Regarding racism, I find it difficult to declare it a top priority when we have recently elected a black president and vice president, when approval of black/white interracial marriage has risen from 4% among whites in 1958 to close to 90% by 2020, and "a number of empirically minded social scientists have pointed out that racism appears to be declining by any objective standard" (Wilfred Reilly, "Testing the Tests for Racism," Academic Questions, Fall 2021).

Feel free to disagree, as always. One challenge we do not have, at least not yet (despite certain stirrings of thought suppression), is the freedom to disagree.

The America we are leaving It's probably never been more important to ask: What kind of country do I want to live in, work in, and raise my family in? What kind of America do I envision? What is at danger of breaking down?

THE AMERICA WE LEAVE

America's Most Serious Problems: Progressivism vs. Conservatism

Conservatives say that people should have choices. Progressives believe that one political solution fits everyone. The three key differences between being a conservative and a progressive.

The Most Important Issue in America: Health Care

The majority of Americans believe that the United States' health-care system needs change. What many people disagree on is the proper way to go about it.

America's Most Serious Problem: Immigration

Immigration is one of the important building blocks that contribute to America's uniqueness. However, the debate over border security and immigration has become poisoned because politicians have prioritized politics above ideas. And sensible Americans are trapped between zealots on both sides. So, what constitutes a fair strategy for American immigration reform? It walks us through four guiding themes to keep us focused on what is best for all Americans, both now and in the future.

The Most Serious Issues in America: Religious Freedom

"Congress shall make no law respecting the establishment of religion, or prohibiting the free exercise thereof," states the first amendment to the United States constitution. After more than 250 years, religious freedom is still one of the most pressing issues in American culture. This article examines some of the issues underlying this debate and how, in the end, religious freedom benefits everyone.

The Biggest Issues in America: Marriage

Families are the foundations of society. They are personal encounters, yet they have a significant impact on and serve the public good. Strong families build strong communities. Family breakdown, on the other hand, harms society as a whole. That is why America's declining marriage rate is a major source of worry. It is an undeniable fact that when parents marry and families stay together, the best opportunities for financial success, emotional well-being, and good health for both parents and children develop.

America's Most Serious Problem: Education

American schools and colleges are failing in one of their most essential missions: providing students with the skills necessary for a career. How to reduce the rapid rise in both college tuition and student debt by removing the federal government from the student loan market.

Environmental Concerns in the United States

We are being informed that we only have 12 years to address climate change, and the solution is to fundamentally damage the free market system. That means Washington decides how we generate energy, what food we eat, and what kind of cars we drive. The point is, would their solutions work even if we accepted their dire predictions? This article debunks several environmental fallacies and discusses how America can secure inexpensive, dependable, and greener energy by keeping our economy booming.

America's Most Serious Problems: Spending

Despite their promises, politicians continue to spend hundreds of billions of dollars more than the government collects. Every year, they charge it to the national credit card, increasing the debt. That cost now averages $67,000 for each and every American. That's roughly $250,000 for a family of three. It is not too late to save America's incredible potential. But first, we must urge political leaders to stop their reckless spending and set budget constraints.

America's Most Serious Problems: Welfare

When President Lyndon B. Johnson launched his War on Poverty in the 1960s, he declared his intention to eradicate poverty in America. However, after more than five decades, several welfare regimes, and $25 trillion, the aid system has mostly failed the poor. Currently, the United States spends about a trillion dollars each year on over 90 different federal, state, and local welfare programs. Nonetheless, around 12% of Americans are classified as impoverished. We surely spend a lot of money, but how come we still have such a high poverty rate?

THE SOLUTION

The Solutions to America's Seven Biggest Problems for We, the People I write to encourage leaders to embrace facts, humanitarian principles, principled pragmatism, and stark realism as we face unprecedented global upheavals.

"We, the People of the United States, do ordain and establish this Constitution for the United States of America in order to form a more perfect Union, establish Justice, insure domestic tranquillity, provide for the common defense, promote the general welfare, and secure to ourselves and our posterity the blessings of Liberty."

The FATEs (Five Fatalities)

Five transforming factors will determine our species 'fate:

The underlying thesis is that we are divided and paralyzed as a nation by deep, cynical, fully paid for partisanship at a time when the consequences of deferring pragmatic decisions to satisfy the Five Fates could not be higher. The underlying thesis is that we are divided and paralyzed as a nation by deep, cynical, fully paid for partisanship at a time when the consequences of deferring pragmatic decisions to satisfy the Five Fates could not be higher. What should be done?

We may just wait for a major disaster to demolish our current impasse—who knows, the coronavirus pandemic could be such a disaster. Our suggested solution is a campaign championed by "We, The People"—breaking away from these partisan political interests, seeking and finding our own common ground, and launching a nonviolent political movement unlike any other in our history.

The People's Movement must be founded on New Pragmatism, which seeks realistic answers to our most pressing problems in immigration, national security and foreign policy, regulation, technology, employment, health care, and education. Here are a few starting points:

1. Immigration: We are, by definition, an immigrant nation. Our early immigrants, mostly English, Ulster Scots, Dutch, and Germans, committed our founding sins of decimating Native Americans and enslaving Africans.

Best Travel Insurance Companies

Since the nineteenth century, we have repeated the same pattern of discrimination followed by assimilation as each new group of immigrants arrives and attempts to join our Great American Experiment. The Irish was the first big immigrant group; around one-third of Ireland's population departed in the 1800s, often as indentured servants on ships known as "coffin ships" to work as unskilled labor or to join the Union Army. They were originally perceived as drunkards, fighters, and cheaters, but then as full participants in our society as policemen, firefighters, legislators, performers, and, finally, just Americans.

As the Fed fights inflation, expect slower hiring and job cuts.

Scandinavians arrived in the late nineteenth and early twentieth centuries, followed by Jews and Catholics from Italy, Poland, and other European countries, and finally Christians and fewer Muslims from Lebanon and Syria. Americans inevitably formed anti-immigrant organizations, ranging from the nativist, anti-Catholic Know-Nothing Party in the 1850s through the Chinese Exclusion Act adopted by Congress in 1882 and others.

Since Operation Wetback in 1954, undoubtedly the most significant impediment to US immigration policy has been the flood of Mexicans, both legitimately and illegally, and our unequal reaction of welcome and rejection. Much less recognized is the massive increase in overall immigration since the beginning of the twentieth century, from less than 20 million immigrants in the United States in 1990 to over 44 million today—roughly 13.7% of our total population. Mexico accounts for over 12 million immigrants, with over 2 million coming from India, China, and the Philippines. Many more come from Asian and Latin American nations.

Immigration Diagram

These movements are mostly the result of legislation enacted by Congress. However, our last really comprehensive immigration law was passed over 50 years ago, with the Immigration and Nationality Act Amendments of 1965 (the Hart-Celler Act), which included the problematic preference for immigrants with U.S. citizen family links.

We have managed to convert immigration, the source of much of our nation's vitality, prosperity, and creativity, into an angry, cruel, dividing issue about walls and race as a consequence of our own actions and policies. and sending away talented, hardworking people that any country would welcome as citizens.

"We, the Individuals," need to design a comprehensive immigration policy that represents our nation's interests, stimulates the immigration of people with needed talents, maintains the vitality and cultural thriving that comes from a varied community, and embraces our American principles of social justice. We must recognize that, as a nation-state, America, too, must limit how many new immigrants may come here and who they are.

In terms of national security, military, and foreign policy, Vietnam, Grenada, Panama, Kuwait, Kosovo, Iraq, Afghanistan, and Somalia rank second. In terms of national security, military, and foreign policy, Vietnam, Grenada, Panama, Kuwait, Kosovo, Iraq, Afghanistan, and Somalia rank second. What is our national strategy and policy for the deployment of large armed forces? forces? Is the decision-making relationship between our diplomatic, military, executive, and legislative departments of government appropriate for today's world? Do we want to be the "preferred national security partner" of NATO's now 27 European members?

members? Is Putin an antagonist or a role model for our president? Will we continue to play the role of "friendly cop" for China's natural adversaries in Asia, such as Japan, South Korea, Taiwan, and India? Are we ready for a cyberwar? cyberwar? War in Space?

Survey our nation's best practitioners and strategists from across the political spectrum, and you'll find a strong, basic belief that we need a pragmatic, bipartisan national security and foreign policy that is firmly grounded in our long-term national interests.

Baghdad's security has been beefed up as the violence continues.

When distinguished leaders like Colin Powell vote to support invading Iraq based on blurry photos of WMDs, and James Matthis resigns because "[President Trump] has the right to have a Secretary of Defense whose views are better aligned with yours...", it is clear that we lack a coherent approach to these high-stakes decisions, and we are well past the need for a fundamental reset in our national security and foreign policy.

What should be done? done? A National Security and Foreign Policy Commission Robert Gates and Leon

Panetta serve as co-chairs. Where the likes of Henry Kissinger, George Schultz, Colin Powell, Condeleeza Rice, Madeleine Albright, James Baker may still give their significant ideas. ideas. Who is going to commission it? We are the people.

We will also dispatch a rocketship with Hillary Clinton, Dick Cheney, Donald Rumsfeld, and Jared Kushner, who have been tasked with preparing a white paper on the possibility of a space war with cosmic invaders.

Just one more thing. We the People support a two-year national service program for all people under the age of 25. Military service is, of course, a choice, but we will let our military choose people they feel are qualified. Other events will primarily focus on allowing all young American adults to get to know one another as we develop our communities at the local level. Other events will primarily focus on allowing all young American adults to get to know one another as we develop our communities at the local level.

3. Regulators: "Deregulate" is a conservative crowd-pleaser. This constant mantra—or shout—from politicians to the business community is akin to a babysitter telling a family of pre-adolescents, "I'm going to the movies." However, by oversimplification, it

intentionally obscures the facts. Every industry in America is heavily regulated. "In whose interests do we regulate?" asks the question. "Deregulate" is actually code for "Regulate only in the interests of business." And businesses, which are neither saints nor sinners, will be willing collaborators in pursuing their own goals.

In general, deregulation leads to fossil fuel companies polluting more during production and use. And financial institutions, which can conceal more than they reveal, take risks that end badly...for us.

Instead, regulation should largely be focused on We, The People as consumers and customers, those on the weak end of asymmetrical information and power. Let us simplify regulation for fossil fuel businesses while reducing pollution for us, the people, via a carbon price (more later). Let's face it: most of us have no or little understanding of the terms of our mortgage or 401(k) account. We, the People, should demand regulation that prioritizes our national well-being above the interests of the corporate sector.

4. Technology: Living and working in Silicon Valley, it is not contentious to say that we are in the Second Internet Bubble, with the inevitable collapse being disregarded. The first Internet bubble provided us

basically understandable stuff... Amazon and eBay offered everything to everybody and everyone. Travel services are available online. We already knew that Apple offered laptops and other amazing gadgets. And, as usual, Microsoft marketed software to both individuals and enterprises. Google was founded in 1998, but its advertising business model did not take off until many years later.

But, since Mark Zuckerberg launched Facemash at Harvard in 2003, we've been so taken with...or is it semi-addicted to...our new technologies that we've forgotten to consider how they're affecting us as individuals, families, communities, and as a society. And now, with facial recognition and the creation of massive data bases pulled from many sources, we are getting our first sense of what the superpower of non-human-centered AI might bring to our world.

Here is a starting point for We, The People to adopt as we finally get around to regulating the technology industry in our best interests:

To register for any social media or other technology account, simple identification data must be provided. Name, address, social security, drivers license. No anonymous terrorists. Or cyberbullies. Or unwelcome photos or shaming. (If you are thinking this is a bad idea, think about why.)

All social media platforms and other technologies must have a subscription pricing model that enables users to pay for the service while opting out of advertising and disclosing personal information.

The Justice Department's Antitrust Division should return from its decade-long hiatus.

This will be a decades-long struggle involving billions of dollars of investment, which only large corporations and two nations, the United States and China, can afford. Fortunately, if we wake up now and develop a consumer-oriented regulatory scheme, we, the people, will be able to ensure that we have the strongest technology companies while limiting the damage these products cause to our society. However, how and how often you use your gadgets is entirely up to you.

CHAPTER SIX

THE WORLD IS

'DANGEROUSLY

IRREVERSIBLE'

The world is on the verge of irreversible climate change. Scientists are kept awake at night by these five critical points.

Five years ago, the United Nations' panel on climate change was tasked with producing a series of reports outlining the science behind the phenomenon, its effects on the planet, and how humanity might save itself.

The most recent of these reports arrived this week, and the news is bleak. The world's scientists say the crisis is upon us, and unless we act now, multiple crucial planetary systems are on the cusp of permanent damage.

"We can't kick this can down the road any longer," said Andrea Dutton, a geoscientist at the University of Wisconsin, Madison.

According to NASA, the Earth's temperature has increased by more than 2 degrees since the 1880s. That may not appear to be much, but it is enough to disrupt natural systems that support all living things, including humans.

U.N. Secretary-General António Guterres warned in a blistering address Monday that the globe is "dangerously close to tipping points that might lead to cascading and irreversible" repercussions.

Here are five tipping points that experts believe will occur in our children's lifetimes:

The Amazon rainforest is transformed into a savanna.

The Amazon rainforest is in the most immediate danger.

The 2.5 million square mile rainforest is so vast it creates its own rainfall and is home to 10% of the world's species.

But rising temperatures and increasing drought are bringing it ever closer to crossing the threshold from lush rainforest to arid savannah.

"The recent evidence has been quite alarming. "It really does look like we're closing in on a place where a relatively modest amount of drying could kill off the rainforest and turn it into something else," said Daniel Swain, a climate scientist at the University of California, Los Angeles.

In part due to the rising heat and lack of rain, the Amazon is witnessing more flames. These devastate vast regions, which regenerate as grasslands with few trees rather than rainforests. Illegal logging to produce grass or soybeans to feed livestock worsens the situation.

A study released last month discovered indicators of lost habitat in more than 75% of the rainforest since the early 2000s. According to a 2020 report, up to 40% of the surviving rainforest may not regenerate if destroyed.

Coral reefs are dying.

Coral reefs are in jeopardy.

Corals are critical to ocean health. They are home to at least a quarter of all marine species while covering just 0.2% of the ocean bottom. They protect baby fish and house tiny creatures and fish that provide food for bigger fish. According to scientists, coral reefs account for 25% of all fish harvested in poor nations.

Coral reefs can only thrive in a rather small temperature range. The algae that live in the tissues of the corals that create them provide a large portion of their diet. When exposed to excessively warm seawater, the coral's stress response is to expel algae, causing the coral to turn white. Coral bleaching is a natural process that can turn a thriving ecosystem into a cemetery of dead shells if it lasts too long.

According to a report published last year, nearly 15% of the world's reefs have vanished since 2009, owing primarily to climate change.

"They're being burned to death," said Dutton, a MacArthur Genius Award recipient who studies the ocean's ancient past.

"The frequency with which these bleaching episodes are occurring astounds those of us who study them," she added. "It will have a massive domino impact on marine systems and on humanity."

Melting ice sheets

The world's biggest ice sheets are running out of time.

The Antarctic and Greenland ice sheets are both melting, with the Antarctic being the most vulnerable.

If they completely melted, global sea levels would increase dramatically. The loss of the Antarctic ice sheet could result in a rise of up to 11 feet. According to Timothy Lenton, chair of climate change and Earth system science at the University of Exeter in the United Kingdom, the loss of the Greenland ice sheet could be 23 feet.

"About 90% of the transportation globally travels across the ocean, and all port infrastructure is at sea level—you can see what a problem this will pose," said Peter Schlosser, head of the Global Futures Laboratory at Arizona State University.

Though the increase presumably will take considerably longer, it might happen as early as 100 years from now for Antarctica and 300 years for Greenland, a report by Lenton found.

"I realize that may sound far off, but you'd be talking about needing to relocate numerous coastal megacities in the next 100 or 150 years," he added.

The Atlantic circulation is halted.

The Atlantic's circulation is jeopardized.

The Atlantic Thermohaline Circulation Collapse is the official name for this threat. If it were to happen, it could bring about an ice age in Europe and a sea level rise in cities like Boston and New York.

What's known as the Atlantic Meridional Overturning Circulation (AMOC) keeps warmer water from the tropics flowing north along the coast of northern Europe to the Arctic, where it cools and sinks to the bottom of the ocean. That cooler water is then pulled back southward along the coast of North America as part of a circular pattern.

This cycle keeps northern Europe several degrees warmer than it would otherwise be and brings colder water to the coast of North America.

There is some indication the system has experienced a gradual weakening over the past few decades, and it may be critically unstable.

According to Lenton's findings, if global temperatures continue to climb, the AMOC might collapse in 50 to 250 years.

According to the 2019 IPCC assessment, the AMOC will "very likely" decrease this century, although it has a less than 10% risk of collapsing.

However, the lack of a regular flow of warmer water into Europe might drop temperatures there, enhance storms, and raise sea levels near North America's northeastern shore.

"Because you're not transferring as much water, it backs up down the East Coast," Dutton said.

The "snow woodland" vanishes.

The huge boreal forests of the north will become treeless grasslands in the future.

Cold-weather woods in the Western United States, Canada, and Alaska are thought to store more than 30% of the world's forest carbon. Huge volumes of greenhouse gases would be released into the environment if they did not exist, increasing global warming.

It is being destroyed by a mixture of three factors: heat, fire, and bark bugs. Rising temperatures exacerbate droughts and increase the likelihood of forest fires. Heat also increases the number of bark beetles, which destroys forests.

"Forests can survive heat and drought to a degree, and then there's a threshold where they can't," Swain said. "There's evidence that we're approaching or have passed that stage."

North American bark beetles are native to the continent. They normally spawn once a year in northern latitudes when winters are frigid and summers are cool. They can reproduce twice as much as they can with warmer and shorter winters, resulting in larger populations, more stress, and tree death.

The dead trees pose a fire danger, increasing the size and intensity of wildfires. When the fire is extinguished, grasslands, not forests, can regenerate.

"There are some trees that are well adapted to the harsh cold, but you've made the summers too hot for them," Lenton explained.

The time has come.

Scientists and many international leaders are unambiguous: the moment for action is now. Not next year, not in a decade.

"The stakes are obvious. "Climate warming will have irrevocable and unfathomable consequences for complacency." According to John Kerry, the United States' special presidential envoy on climate change.

Experts argue that any of these collapses, even if not complete, would be harmful to the environment. Worse, when one system becomes unstable, it affects others, resulting in even greater instability and possible collapse. Carbon that is currently stored in the earth's atmosphere would be released into the atmosphere, causing further temperature rise and disaster.

Experts say that in the face of these possibilities, humanity must avoid raising the planet's temperature any further than it already has.

"We're approaching thresholds we don't want to cross," Schlosser said. "We're coming close to the point when the Earth is retaliating against us."

THE UNINHABITABLE

EARTH

Climate change has the potential to cause famine, economic collapse, and a sun that cooks us.

Moving around outside when it's over 105 degrees Fahrenheit would be lethal in Costa Rica's jungles, where humidity routinely exceeds 90%. And the effect would be fast: Within a few hours, a human body would be cooked to death from both inside and out. Fossils by Heartless Machine

I. 'Doomsday'

Looking beyond scientific reluctance

It is, I promise, worse than you think. If your anxiety about global warming is dominated by fears of sea-level rise, you are barely scratching the surface of what terrors are possible, even within the lifetime of a teenager today. Yet, the growing oceans — and the cities they will drown have so dominated our vision of global warming, and so overburdened our capacity for climate alarm, that they have clouded our perception of other risks, many of which are much closer at hand. Rising water is terrible, extremely bad; nonetheless, evacuating the shore will not suffice.

Indeed, unless billions of humans make significant changes in how they live, parts of the Earth will likely become uninhabitable, and other parts will become horrifically inhospitable by the end of this century.

Even when we focus our attention on climate change, we are unable to comprehend its magnitude. This winter, a string of days 60 to 70 degrees warmer than normal baked the North Pole, melting the permafrost that encased Norway's Svalbard seed vault—a global food bank dubbed "Doomsday," designed to ensure that our agriculture survives any disaster, and which appeared to be flooded by climate change less than ten years after it was built.

For the time being, the Doomsday vault is safe: the building has been guarded, and the seeds are protected. However, viewing the incident as a metaphor for impending flooding missed the more important point. Permafrost was previously unimportant to climate scientists because, as the name implies, it was soil that remained permanently frozen. But Arctic permafrost stores 1.8 trillion tons of carbon, more than twice as much as is now floating in the Earth's atmosphere. When it thaws and is released, that carbon may evaporate as methane, which is 34 times as powerful a greenhouse-gas warming blanket as carbon dioxide when measured over a century; it is 86 times as powerful when measured over two decades. In other words, we have twice as much carbon trapped in Arctic permafrost as is currently wreaking havoc on the planet's atmosphere, all of it set to be released at a date that keeps getting pushed back, partially in the form of a gas that multiplies its warming power 86 times over.

Maybe you already know that—there are worrisome stories in the news every day, such as those last month that appeared to imply satellite data showed the world warming more than twice as quickly as scientists had anticipated (in reality, the underlying narrative was significantly less alarming than the headlines) (in fact, the underlying story was considerably less alarming than the headlines). Or the news from Antarctica this past May, when a fracture in an ice shelf developed 11 miles in six days, then continued growing; the break now has only three miles to go — by the time you read this, it may have already reached the open ocean, where it will dump one of the largest icebergs ever into the sea, a process called "calving."

But, no matter how well-informed you are, you are almost certainly not scared enough. Our society has gone apocalyptic with zombie movies and Mad Max dystopias in recent decades, maybe as a consequence of mistaken climate panic, but when it comes to real-world warming problems, we suffer from an astounding lack of innovation. There are several reasons for this: Aversion caused by fear, on the other hand, is a form of denial.

Science fiction exists somewhere between scientific reticence and science. This website represents hundreds of scholarly publications on climate change and is the result of dozens of interviews and conversations with climatologists and experts in related disciplines. What follows is not a series of predictions about what will happen, which will be largely governed by the far less clear science of human reaction. Instead, it reflects our best knowledge of where the world is headed in the absence of meaningful action. It appears unlikely that any of these warming scenarios will be completely realized, owing to the damage that will occur along the way, which will shake our complacency. However, these scenarios, not the actual climate, serve as the baseline. In reality, they are our timeline.

"The Models Are Too Conservative," says a Paleontologist on Climate Change Today.

The present tense of climate change—the devastation we've already baked into our future—is horrifying enough. Most people act as if Miami and Bangladesh have a chance of survival; most of the experts I spoke with believe we'll lose them within a century, even if we stop using fossil fuels in the next decade. Two degrees of warming was once thought to be the tipping point for disaster, releasing tens of millions of climate refugees onto an unprepared planet. According to the Paris climate accords, two degrees is our goal now, and experts only offer us a few options for getting there. The United Nations Intergovernmental Panel on Climate Change publishes periodic reports that are widely regarded as the "gold standard" of climate research; the most recent one predicts four degrees of warming by the beginning of the next century if current trends continue. However, this is only a median projection. The upper end of the probability curve reaches eight degrees — and the authors still haven't figured out how to deal with that permafrost melt. The IPCC assessments also fail to account for the albedo effect (less ice equals less reflected and more absorbed sunlight, resulting in greater warming); increased cloud cover (which traps heat); or the dieback of forests and other plants (which take carbon from the atmosphere) (which extract carbon from the atmosphere). Each of them promises to exacerbate warming, and the history of the planet shows that temperatures can change by up to five degrees Celsius in thirteen years. The oceans were hundreds of feet higher the last time the world was even four degrees warmer, says Peter Brannen in The Ends of the World, his new history of the planet's major extinction disasters.

Before the one we are living through now, the Earth experienced five mass extinctions, each of which erased the evolutionary record so completely that it functioned as a reset of the planetary clock, and many climate scientists believe they are the best analog for the ecological future we are facing. Unless you're a teenager, you've probably read in your high school textbooks that these extinctions were caused by asteroids. In reality, all but the one that wiped out the dinosaurs were caused by climate change caused by greenhouse gases. The most notable occurred 252 million years ago, when carbon warmed the Earth by five degrees, intensified when that warming triggered the release of methane in the Arctic, and resulted in the extinction of 97 percent of all life on Earth. We are now adding carbon to the atmosphere at a far faster rate, at least ten times faster, according to most estimates. The tempo is accelerating. This is what Stephen Hawking meant when he said this spring that the species needs to colonize other planets within the next century to survive, and what prompted Elon Musk to reveal his plans to build a Mars home within the next 40 to 100 years. Of course, these are nonspecialists, and they may be as susceptible to unnecessary fear as you or I. But the numerous sober-minded scientists I met over the past several months—the most qualified and tenured in the field, few of them prone to alarmism, and many advisors to the IPCC who still criticize its conservatism—had silently reached an apocalyptic conclusion, too: No amount of carbon reduction can prevent a climate catastrophe.

When Did Humans Permanently Endanger the Earth?

Over the last few decades, the phrase "Anthropocene" has emerged from academic discourse and into popular consciousness—a name given to the geologic time we now live in and a way to symbolize that it is a new age, demarcated on the wall chart of deep history by human activity. One issue with the term is that it implies a conquering of nature (and even echoes the biblical "dominion"). And, however confident you are that we have already ravaged the natural world, which we undoubtedly have, it is quite another to consider the possibility that we have only provoked it, first in ignorance and then in denial, a climate system that will now go to war with us for many centuries, perhaps until it destroys us. That is what Wallace Smith Broecker, the affable oceanographer who coined the phrase "global warming," means when he refers to the Earth as an "angry beast." You could also use "war machine." We are arming it more and more each day.

II Death from Heat

The Bahraining of New York.

In El Salvador's sugarcane region, up to one-fifth of the population suffers from chronic renal disease, which is said to be the result of dehydration from working crops that were easily harvested just two decades ago. Heartless Machine

Humans, like other animals, are heat engines; survival requires them to constantly cool themselves, much like panting dogs. The temperature must be low enough for the air to act as a refrigerant, drawing heat from the skin to keep the engine running. At seven degrees of warming, that would become impossible for large portions of the planet's equatorial band, particularly the tropics, where humidity adds to the problem; in Costa Rica's jungles, for example, where humidity routinely tops 90 percent, simply moving around outside when it's over 105 degrees Fahrenheit would be lethal. And the result would be swift: within a few hours, a human body would be completely burned from the inside out.

Temperature change Doubters argue that the earth has warmed and cooled many times in the past, but the temperature window that has allowed for human existence is relatively small, even by planetary history standards. At 11 or 12 degrees of warming, more than half of the world's population, as it is presently distributed, would perish from direct heat. Things are unlikely to become so hot this century, but models of unchecked emissions will ultimately lead us there. This century, particularly in the tropics, the pain areas will be squeezed far faster than a seven-degree rise. The key factor is something called wet-bulb temperature, which is a measurement as simple as it sounds: the heat registered on a thermometer wrapped in a damp sock as it's swung around in the air (because moisture evaporates from a sock more quickly in dry air, this single number reflects both heat and humidity). Since the moisture evaporates from a sock more quickly in dry air, this single number reflects both heat and humidity). Most places now have a wet-bulb maximum temperature of 26 or 27 degrees Celsius; the true red line for habitability is 35 degrees. Heat stress occurs much sooner.

Actually, we're nearly there. Since 1980, the number of places experiencing harmful or extreme heat has increased 50-fold; an even greater rise is on the way. The five warmest summers in Europe since 1500 have all occurred since 2002, and the IPCC predicts that simply being outside at that time of year will be detrimental to much of the planet. Even if we meet the Paris targets of two degrees of warming, cities like Karachi and Kolkata will become nearly uninhabitable, with terrible heat waves like the ones that hit them in 2015. At four degrees, the disastrous European heat wave of 2003, which killed up to 2,000 people per day, will be just another summer. According to a National Oceanic and Atmospheric Administration assessment focused solely on effects within the United States, summer labor of any kind would become impossible in the lower Mississippi Valley at six, and everyone east of the Rockies would be subjected to more heat stress than anyone, anywhere in the world today. According to Joseph Romm's authoritative book Climate Change: What Everyone Needs to Know, heat stress in New York City would approach that of present-day Bahrain, one of the world's hottest locations, and the temperature in Bahrain "would induce hyperthermia in even sleeping humans."

Remember that the high-end IPCC estimate is still two degrees warmer. According to the World Bank, by the end of the century, the coldest months in tropical South America, Africa, and the Pacific will be warmer than the hottest months at the end of the twentieth century. Air-conditioning may help, but it will ultimately exacerbate the carbon problem; anyway, even with the climate-controlled malls of the Arab emirates, it is not remotely feasible to air-condition all of the world's hottest regions, many of which are also the poorest. And, without a doubt, the situation will be most serious in the Middle East and the Persian Gulf, where the heat index reached 163 degrees Fahrenheit in 2015. Many decades from now, the hajj will be physically impossible for the 2 million Muslims who make the pilgrimage each year.

It's not just the hajj and Mecca; the heat is already killing us. In El Salvador's sugarcane region, up to one-fifth of the population suffers from chronic renal illness, including more than a quarter of the males, most likely as a result of dehydration from working crops that were easily harvested only two decades ago. Patients on dialysis with renal failure can expect to live for five years; without it, life expectancy is in the weeks. Of course, heat stress threatens to harm us in ways other than our kidneys. It's 121 degrees outside my door as I write this in the California desert in mid-June. It is not a record high.

III. The End of Food

In the tundra, I'm praying for cornfields.

The general rule for staple grain crops grown at optimal temperatures is that for every degree of warming, yields decline by 10%. Some estimates put it at as high as 15% or even 17%. That means that if the world warms by five degrees Celsius by the end of the century, we may have half as many people to feed and half as much food to feed them. And proteins are even worse: it takes 16 calories of grain to produce a single calorie of hamburger meat, which is slaughtered from a cow that has spent its entire life polluting the environment with methane farts.

Plant physiologists will point out that the cereal-crop arithmetic only applies to locations that are already at peak growth temperature, and they are correct—theoretically, a warmer climate will make it easier to produce maize in Greenland. However, as groundbreaking research by Rosamond Naylor and David Battisti has shown, the tropics are already too hot to efficiently grow grain, and the places where grain is produced today are already at optimal growing temperatures — which means that even a small warming will push them down the slope of declining productivity. And you can't just move croplands north a few hundred miles because yields in places like northern Canada and Russia are limited by soil quality; it takes many generations for the earth to develop ideally productive dirt.

Drought may be a bigger concern than heat, with some of the world's most fertile land rapidly turning to desert. Precipitation is notoriously difficult to calculate, but projections for later this century are nearly unanimous: severe droughts nearly everywhere food is now produced. Without significant reductions in emissions, southern Europe will face a persistent catastrophic drought by 2080, far worse than the American dust bowl ever was. The same will be true in Iraq and Syria, as well as most of the rest of the Middle East; some of Australia's, Africa's, and South America's most densely populated areas; and China's breadbasket provinces. None of these regions, which currently produce the majority of the world's food, will be reliable suppliers of any. According to a 2015 NASA study, the droughts in the American plains and Southwest would be worse than any drought in a thousand years—including those that struck between 1100 and 1300, which "dried up all the rivers east of the Sierra Nevada mountains" and may have been responsible for the Anasazi civilization's demise.

Remember, we do not live in a world without hunger as it is. Far from it: most estimates place the global undernourished population at 800 million. In case you haven't heard, this spring has already brought an unprecedented quadruple famine to Africa and the Middle East; the United Nations has warned that different hunger events in Somalia, South Sudan, Nigeria, and Yemen might kill 20 million people this year alone.

IV Climate Disasters IV

What happens after the bubonic ice melts?

Rock, when placed correctly, is a record of planetary history, with periods as long as millions of years squashed by the forces of geological time into strata with amplitudes of only inches, or even less. Ice works similarly as a climatic ledger, but it is also a frozen history, some of which may be reanimated when unfrozen. There are diseases that have been trapped beneath Arctic ice for millions of years—in some cases, since before humans were present to encounter them. As a result, when those ancient diseases emerge from the ice, our immune systems will have no idea how to respond.

The Arctic also has terrible bugs from more recent times. Already, researchers in Alaska have discovered remnants of the 1918 flu pandemic, which infected as many as 500 million people and killed as many as 100 million—roughly 5% of the world's population and nearly six times as many as died in the world war, for which the pandemic served as a kind of gruesome capstone. According to the BBC, experts believe smallpox and the bubonic plague are also frozen in Siberian ice-a shortened history of horrific human diseases laid out like egg salad in the Arctic heat.

Many of these organisms will not survive the thaw, according to experts, who point to the meticulous lab conditions under which they have already reanimated several of them—the 32,000-year-old "extremophile" bacteria revived in 2005, an 8 million-year-old bug brought back to life in 2007, and a 3.5 million-year-old one self-injected out of curiosity—to suggest that those are necessary conditions for the return of such ancient plagues. However, a boy was killed and 20 others were infected by anthrax released when retreating permafrost exposed the frozen carcass of a reindeer killed by the bacteria at least 75 years earlier; 2,000 modern reindeer were also infected, carrying and spreading the disease beyond the tundra.

What worries epidemiologists more than ancient illnesses are current scourges that have been moved, rewired, or even re-evolved as a result of warming. The first factor is geography. Prior to the early-modern era, when daring sailboats expedited the mixing of people and their bugs, human provinciality served as an antidote to epidemics. Even with globalization and the great intermingling of human populations, our ecosystems are generally stable today, and this serves as another border, but global warming will jumble those ecosystems and allow sickness to cross those boundaries as confidently as Cortés did. If you live in Maine or France, you don't have to be concerned about dengue or malaria. But you will when the tropics move north and mosquitoes accompany them. You weren't concerned about Zika a few years ago, either.

As it happens, Zika may be a good illustration of the second troubling effect: disease mutation. One reason you hadn't heard of Zika until recently is that it was trapped in Uganda; another is that it did not appear to cause birth problems until recently. Scientists are still not sure what happened or what they missed. But there are some things we do know for certain about how the environment affects various diseases: Malaria, for example, thrives in hotter environments not only because the insects that transmit it do, but also because the parasite reproduces 10 times faster for every degree of increase in temperature. That is one of the reasons why the World Bank predicts that 5.2 billion people will be affected by it by 2050.

V. Suffocating Air:

a deadly cloud that suffocates millions of people.

The coldest months in tropical South America, Africa, and the Pacific are expected to be warmer than the warmest months at the end of the twentieth century by the end of the century. Photographer: Heartless Machine

Our lungs need oxygen, yet it is just a small part of what we breathe. Carbon dioxide is becoming more prevalent. It just surpassed 400 parts per million, and high-end forecasts based on current trends indicate it will reach 1,000 ppm by 2100. When compared to the air we now breathe, human cognitive performance is reduced by 21% at that concentration.

Other things in the hotter air are even more concerning, with even minor increases in pollution having the potential to shorten people's lives by ten years. The more the globe warms, the more ozone forms, and by mid-century, the National Center for Atmospheric Research estimates that Americans will face a 70% increase in dangerous ozone pollution. By 2090, up to 2 billion people worldwide will be breathing air that exceeds the WHO "safe" limit; one paper this month demonstrated that, among other effects, a pregnant mother's exposure to ozone increases the child's risk of autism (up to tenfold, depending on other environmental factors) (as much as tenfold, combined with other environmental factors). Which makes you think about the autism epidemic in West Hollywood once again.

Already, more than 10,000 people die each day from the tiny particles produced by fossil-fuel combustion; each year, 339,000 people die from wildfire smoke, in part because climate change has extended the forest-fire season (in the United States, it has increased by 78 days since 1970). According to the US Forest Service, wildfires will be twice as destructive as they are today by 2050, with the area burned potentially expanding fivefold in certain areas. What concerns people the most is the effect it would have on emissions, especially if the flames decimate peat bog forests. More peatland fires in Indonesia, for example, boosted world CO2 emissions by up to 40% in 1997, and more burning merely means more heat, which means more burning. There's also the terrifying possibility that rain forests like the Amazon, which experienced their second "hundred-year drought" in five years in 2010, will dry out enough to become vulnerable to these kinds of devastating, rolling forest fires, which will not only release massive amounts of carbon into the atmosphere but will also shrink the forest's size. This is especially alarming given that the Amazon alone supplies 20% of our oxygen.

Then there's the more well-known kind of pollution. Melting Arctic ice disrupted Asian weather patterns in 2013, robbing industrial China of the natural ventilation systems to which it had become used, and coating much of the country's north in unbreathable smog. It was literally unbreathable. The Air Quality Index categorizes the risks and warns of "serious aggravation of heart or lung disease and premature mortality in people with cardiopulmonary disease and the elderly" and "serious risk of respiratory effects" for everyone else; at that level, "everyone should avoid all outdoor exertion." The 2013 Chinese "air pocalypse" peaked at what would have been an air quality index of more than 800. Pollution was responsible for one-third of all deaths in the country that year.

VI **Endless War.**

The violence was baked into the heat.

When it comes to Syria, climatologists are cautious. They want you to know that, although climate change did cause a drought that led to civil war, it is not entirely accurate to state that the violence was caused by warming; Lebanon, for example, had similar crop failures. However, researchers such as Marshall Burke and Solomon Hsiang have quantified some of the less evident links between temperature and violence: Scientists think that for every half-degree of warming, civilizations will face a 10% to 20% increase in the likelihood of armed conflict. Nothing in climate science is simple, but the math is terrifying: A five-degree-warmer planet would have half as many wars as we have today. Overall, social conflict is expected to more than treble this century.

This is one of the reasons, as almost every climate scientist I spoke with pointed out, why the United States military is obsessed with climate change: The drowning of all American Navy bases due to sea-level rise is difficult enough, but being the world's policeman becomes much more difficult when the crime rate doubles. In fact, climate change has not just led to conflict in Syria. Some claim that the rising level of violence in the Middle East over the past generation reflects the effects of global warming, which is especially unpleasant considering that warming began to accelerate when the industrialized world extracted and then burned the region's oil.

What explains the relationship between climate change and conflict? Some of it is due to agriculture and economics; much of it is due to forced migration, which is already at an all-time high, with at least 65 million displaced people roaming the globe right now. But there's also the simple fact of individual annoyance. Heat increases municipal crime rates, as does profanity on social media, and there's a chance that a major-league pitcher, returning to the field after a teammate is hurt by a pitch, may strike an opposing batter in retaliation. And the introduction of air conditioning in the developed world in the mid-twentieth century did little to alleviate the summer crime epidemic.

VII. Indefinite Economic Collapse:

Poor capitalism in a half-poor world.

The murmuring mantra of global neoliberalism, which thrived between the Cold War's conclusion and the onset of the Great Recession, is that economic progress will save us from everything. The murmuring mantra of global neoliberalism, which thrived between the Cold War's conclusion and the onset of the Great Recession, is that economic progress will save us from everything.

However, in the aftermath of the 2008 crash, a growing number of historians studying "fossil capitalism" have begun to argue that the entire history of rapid economic growth, which began somewhat abruptly in the 18th century, is the result of our discovery of fossil fuels and all their raw power — a one-time injection of new "value" into a system that had previously been characterized by gynecological stagnation. gynecological stagnation. Nobody lived better than their parents, grandparents, or ancestors from 500 years ago, unless it was in the immediate aftermath of a terrible epidemic like the Black Death, which allowed the lucky survivors to suck up the resources released by mass graves. These scholars predict that after all fossil fuels have been depleted, the world economy will return to a "steady state." Of course, that one-time investment carries a significant long-term cost: climate change.

The most compelling research on the economics of warming has also come from Hsiang and his colleagues, who are not historians of fossil capitalism but provide some fairly pessimistic predictions: Every degree Celsius of global warming costs the economy 1.2 percent of GDP (an amazing figure, given that we consider growth in the low single digits to be "strong").This is excellent research, and their median forecast is for a 23% drop in global per capita earnings by the end of the century (due to changes in agriculture, crime, storms, energy, mortality, and labor) (resulting from changes in agriculture, crime, storms, energy, mortality, and labor). This is excellent research, and their median forecast is for a 23% drop in global per capita earnings by the end of the century (due to changes in agriculture, crime, storms, energy, mortality, and labor) (resulting from changes in agriculture, crime, storms, energy, mortality, and labor).

Tracing the probability curve's shape is more scary: Climate change, they say, has a 12% chance of reducing world output by more than 50% by 2100 and a 51% chance of reducing per capita GDP by 20% or more by then unless emissions are reduced. In comparison, the Great Recession reduced global GDP by around 6% in a one-time shock; Hsiang and his colleagues estimate a one-in-eight chance of an eight-fold worse ongoing and permanent effect by the end of the century.

The magnitude of such economic ruin is difficult to comprehend, but consider what the world would look like today if the economy were half as large, producing half as much value and providing half as much to the world's workers. It makes the grounding of flights out of Phoenix last month seem like a pathetically small economic problem. And, among other things, it renders the premise of postponing government action on carbon reductions in favor of relying only on growth and technology to address the problem a nonsensical business calculation. And, among other things, it renders the premise of postponing government action on carbon reductions in favor of relying only on growth and technology to address the problem a nonsensical business calculation.

Keep in mind that every round-trip ticket from New York to London costs the Arctic three square meters of ice.

VIII. Poisoned Oceans

Sulfide burps off the skeleton shore

It is a given that the water will turn into a killer. We will suffer at least four feet of sea-level rise by the end of the century unless emissions are significantly reduced. A third of the world's largest cities are located on the coast, not to mention its power plants, ports, naval bases, farmlands, fisheries, river deltas, marshlands, and rice-paddy empires, and even those above ten feet will flood far more quickly and often if the sea level rises that high. Today, at least 600 million people live within 10 meters of the water.

But the flooding of their homelands is only the beginning. More than a third of the world's carbon is currently being absorbed by the oceans, which is a good thing since otherwise we'd have that much more heat already. However, the result is "ocean acidification," which may add half a degree of warming this century on its own. It is already destroying the planet's water basins, which you may recall as the location where life originally appeared. You've probably heard about "coral bleaching," or coral dying, which is sad news since reefs support up to a quarter of all marine life and provide food for half a billion people. Scientists aren't sure how to predict the effects of the stuff we haul out of the ocean to eat, but they do know that in acidic waters, oysters and mussels struggle to grow their shells, and that when the pH of human blood drops as much as the pH of the oceans has over the last generation, it induces seizures, comas, and sudden death.

That is not the only effect of ocean acidification. Carbon absorption may set off a feedback loop in which unoxygenated waters develop various bacteria that make the water even more "anoxic," initially in deep ocean "dead zones" and then gradually ascending to the top. There, the small fish perish from lack of oxygen, allowing oxygen-eating bacteria to proliferate, and the feedback loop begins again. This process, in which dead zones spread like cancers, choking off marine life and destroying fisheries, is already well underway in parts of the Gulf of Mexico and just off Namibia, where hydrogen sulfide is bubbling out of the sea along a thousand-mile stretch of land known as the "Skeleton Coast." The name initially referred to the trash of the whaling industry, but it is today more relevant than ever. Because hydrogen sulfide is so toxic, nature has trained humans to detect even the slightest amounts of it, which is why our noses are so adept at detecting farts. Hydrogen sulfide is also the gas that finally killed humankind; as all the feedback loops were engaged and the whirling jet streams of a rising ocean came to a halt, 97 percent of all species on Earth died- it's the planet's preferred gas for a natural holocaust. The ocean's dead zones gradually spread, killing marine species that had dominated the oceans for hundreds of millions of years, and the gas emitted by the inert waters into the atmosphere poisoned everything on land. Plants, as well. It took millions of years for the seas to recover.

IX he Great Filter

Our present unease cannot last.

So how come we can't see it? Amitav Ghosh, an Indian novelist, wonders in his recent book-length essay The Great Derangement why global warming and natural disasters haven't become major subjects of contemporary fiction why we don't seem to be able to imagine climate catastrophe, and why we haven't yet had a spate of novels in the genre he basically imagines into half-existence and calls "the environmental uncanny." "Think about the stories that form around questions like, 'Where were you when the Berlin Wall fell?' or 'Where were you on 9/11?' ,'" he continues. "Will it ever be possible to ask, 'Where were you at 400 ppm?' or 'Where were you when the Larsen B ice shelf broke up?'" His response: Probably not, since the problems and tragedies of climate change are just incompatible with the kinds of stories we tell ourselves about ourselves, especially in novels, which emphasize the journey of an individual conscience rather than the poisonous miasma of communal destiny.

This ignorance will not persist Because the world we are about to enter will not allow it. In a six-degree-warmer world, the Earth's ecosystem will be rife with so many natural disasters that we will simply refer to them as "weather": a constant swarm of out-of-control typhoons, tornadoes, floods, and droughts, the planet will be planet will be regularly assaulted by climate events that have previously destroyed entire civilizations. Hurricanes will become more frequent, necessitating the creation of new categories to categorize them; tornadoes will get longer and wider, striking much more often; and hail rocks will quadruple in size. Humans used to observe the weather to predict the future; in the future, we shall see the retribution of the past in its anger. Early naturalists waxed lyrical about "deep time," the sense they felt when admiring the beauty of this valley or that rock basin of nature's inexorable slowness. What awaits us is more akin to what Victorian anthropologists dubbed "dreamtime" or "everywhen": the semi-mythical experience reported by Aboriginal Australians of witnessing an out-of-time past, when ancestors, heroes, and demigods filled an epic stage. It's already visible in footage of an iceberg collapsing into the sea — a sense of history happening all at once.

It is. Many people see climate change as a sort of moral and economic debt that has accumulated since the beginning of the Industrial Revolution and is now due after several centuries — an interesting point of view, given that the carbon-burning processes that began in 18th-century England lit the fuse for everything that followed. However, more than half of the carbon that humanity has exhaled into the atmosphere in its entire history has been emitted in the last three decades, with the figure increasing to 85 percent since World War II's end. However, more than half of the carbon that humanity has exhaled into the atmosphere in its entire history has been emitted in the last three decades, with the figure increasing to 85 percent since World War II's end. That is, global warming has led us to the edge of planetary disaster in the span of a single generation, and the tale of the industrial world's kamikaze mission is also the story of a single lifetime. For example, my father was born in 1938, and among his earliest memories were the news of Pearl Harbor and the mythic Air Force of the propaganda films that followed, films that doubled as advertisements for imperial-American industrial might; and among his last memories were the coverage of the desperate signing of the Paris climate accords on cable news, ten weeks before he died of lung cancer last July. Or my mother's: born in 1945 to German Jews fleeing the smokestacks where their family were burned, she is now 72 years old and living in an American commodities paradise fed by the supply networks of an industrialized developing world. Or my mother's: born in 1945 to German Jews fleeing the smokestacks where their family were burned, she is now 72 years old and living in an American commodities paradise fed by the supply networks of an industrialized developing world. She has smoked unfiltered for 57 of those years.

Or even the scientists. Some of the men who first observed a changing environment (and, given the age, those who rose to prominence were men) are still alive; a few are still working. Wally Broecker, 84, commutes from the Upper West Side to the Lamont-Doherty Earth Observatory across the Hudson every day. He, like the majority of experts who initially sounded the alarm, thinks that no amount of carbon reduction can help escape tragedy. Instead, he believes in carbon capture, an untested technology for extracting carbon dioxide from the atmosphere that Broecker estimates will cost at least several trillion dollars, and various forms of "geoengineering," a catch-all term for a variety of moon-shot technologies that are far-fetched enough that many climate scientists prefer to regard them as science fiction dreams, or nightmares. He is particularly interested in the aerosol approach, which involves dispersing so much sulfur dioxide into the atmosphere that when it converts to sulfuric acid, it clouds a fifth of the horizon and reflects back 2% of the sun's rays, giving the planet at least a little wiggle room in terms of heat. "Of course, that would turn our sunsets bright red, bleach the sky, and cause more acid rain," he explains. "However, you must consider the gravity of the circumstances." "You must be careful not to say that the giant problem should not be solved because the solution causes some minor problems." He said he wouldn't be there to witness it. "However, in your lifetime..."

Jim Hansen is another godfather from this generation. Born in 1941, he became a climatologist at the University of Iowa, developed the ground breaking "Zero Model" for projecting climate change, and later became NASA's head of climate research, only to leave under pressure when, while still a federal employee, he filed a lawsuit against the federal government charging inaction on climate change (along the way, he was arrested a few times for protesting, too). The lawsuit, brought by a group called Our Children's Trust and often referred to as "kids versus climate change," is based on an argument that the government is violating the equal-protection clause by failing to act on climate change and imposing massive costs on future generations; it is set to be heard this winter in Oregon district court. Hansen has abandoned his favored strategy of fixing the climate issue via a carbon tax and has begun estimating the overall cost of the additional measure of removing carbon from the atmosphere. atmosphere.

Hansen began his career studying Venus, which was once a very Earth-like planet with plenty of life-supporting water before runaway climate change rapidly transformed it into an arid and uninhabitable sphere enveloped in an unbreathable gas; by 30, he was wondering why he should be squinting across the solar system to investigate rapid environmental change when he could see it all around him on the planet he was standing on. "When we wrote our first paper on this in 1981," he told me, "I remember saying to one of my co-authors, 'This is going to be very interesting; we're going to see these things begin to happen sometime during our careers.'

Several of the scientists I spoke with proposed global warming as a solution to Fermi's famous paradox, which asks, "If the universe is so vast, how come we haven't found any other intelligent life in it?" They proposed that a civilization's natural life span may be only a few thousand years, and that an industrial civilization's life span may be only a few hundred. They proposed that a civilization's natural life span may be only a few thousand years, and that an industrial civilization's life span may be only a few hundred. In a cosmos many billions of years old, with star systems separated by time as well as distance, civilizations may begin, flourish, and die far too quickly to ever find one another. "The Great Filter," as Peter Ward, a renowned paleontologist (a charismatic) who was among those responsible for establishing that greenhouse gases were to blame for the planet's catastrophic extinctions, refers to this: "Civilizations arise, but there's an environmental filter that causes them to die out soon," he said. "If you look at planet Earth in the past, the filtering we've had has been in these enormous extinctions." The current mass extinction has just started; much more death is on the way.

Despite this, Ward is an optimist. So are Broecker, Hansen, and many of the other scientists I interviewed. We haven't developed much of a religion of meaning around climate change that could provide comfort or purpose in the face of possible annihilation. But climate scientists have a peculiar faith: we will find a way to prevent extreme warming because we must.

However, Musk is empathetic. And the belief is that longtermism offers a rationalization for brutal commercial methods for techno-optimist CEOs like Musk. Tesla, for example, is well-known for violating labor laws. While union busting may reduce workers' well-being in the short term, it may also reduce Tesla's labor costs, allowing Tesla to lower its prices, hastening the transition to electric vehicles, reducing carbon emissions and creating a more hospitable planet for the hundreds of billions of humans yet to come.

I don't know anything about Tesla or their working conditions in particular, but I do strongly detest the "you've had to break a few eggs" argument. Strong longtermism isn't a claim about goals justifying means; it's just suggesting that it's best to emphasize the long-term implications of your activities when you're not infringing anyone's rights.

The issue is, however, which interests constitute inalienable rights. Longtermism may not excuse performing active injury in order to help future generations, but it certainly supports passive harm, doesn't it? To put it another way, it argues for reallocating some limited resources away from the global poor and toward averting hypothetical future hazards, correct?

That is correct.

So, if it's legal to take possibly lifesaving money from the world's impoverished today in order to benefit future generations, why wouldn't union busting be?

I suppose the key issue is simply what you think about union busting.

Whatever one's views about that specific issue, I believe most of us acknowledge that there are actions that are both somewhat harmful and do not get to the level of human rights violations. So, why would causing little harm be considered unethical yet taking money away from the poor is?

So, on one hand, you have one person drowning and ten people trapped in a burning structure. Who do you help? It's like, "All right, you save the ten." Okay, now a new thinking experiment: You can save the ten from the flames, but you'll have to drown someone—you'll have to tread on their head or something. That seems counterintuitive.

So why not?

because you're using someone as a tool.

I see. As a result, you have a diverse moral portfolio in which you subscribe to utilitarianism to some extent while also adhering to a rights-based deontological ethics that prevents you from stepping on people's heads.

Yes, precisely. However, the situation that a philanthropist faces is somewhat different. There are a million concerns in the world, and you must choose which ones to emphasize. Every dollar I spend to save people from dying of malaria is a dollar I don't spend to save others from tuberculosis or AIDS. As a consequence, there are often recognizable people who have perished as a result of your decision to favor one over the other.

If we're spending resources to avert the next epidemic, we're not using them to distribute bed nets. Joe Biden's recent donation to eliminate student debt might have bought a lot of bed nets and saved a lot of lives. I'm not debating if anything is good or bad. All I'm saying is that there is always an opportunity cost. It's simply an unfortunate part of life that we have to make such judgments.

Some members of the EA community believe that longtermists have underestimated the opportunity costs of their undertakings. Effective altruists frequently calculate the "expected value" of a given donation when evaluating the efficacy of various charities; basically, they take the probability of an initiative's success and an estimate of the total good that the initiative would do if it did succeed and multiply them together.

Skeptics argue that longtermists have simply gamed the formula: since the number of future people is so high, every intervention — even those with a very low chance of success — ends up having a huge "expected value." Indeed, in recent research, you suggested that contributing $10,000 to programs that reduce the likelihood of an AI disaster by merely "0.001%" would yield orders of magnitude more "anticipated" benefit than donating the same amount to anti-malaria projects.

However, when EAs evaluate a charity that helps real people in the present, their likelihood estimates are often based on tangible facts, such as random-control trials examining a charity's impacts in the past. In contrast, the probability estimates you've supplied for both the threat of a superintelligent AI destroying civilisation—and the likelihood that any one effort would prevent such an outcome—are arguably based on nothing more than subjective intuitions. Those intuitions may come from people working in similar fields, but it's not clear that working in AI renders one capable of objectively assessing its potential future worth. You may see this experience as biasing one toward overestimation; people like to believe that the work they do is truly important.

I'd want to add three points to it. First, I don't think "people are likely to inflate the relevance of the kind of work that they perform" is a persuasive complaint in this scenario, particularly given that so many of the EAs who are concerned about AI — maybe even the majority — have no experience in AI. They were just won over by the arguments. That is correct for me. Second, it's not only a matter of intuition. To some extent, we must rely on professional opinions. According to machine-learning specialists, there is a better than 50% chance of human-level artificial intelligence in 37 years, and the danger of calamity as severe as extinction is just around 5%. That's a start. You may also look at the trajectory of computing power through time, where the most powerful machine-learning models now have the processing capacity of an insect brain. Given what we know about neurology, it looks like in around ten years, AI models will have computing power comparable to that of a human brain. So, the intuition is not completely unfounded.

And we simply cannot rely on hard data to make all of the important decisions we must make. We cannot conduct random-control trials to assess how to respond to Russia's invasion of Ukraine. "Okay, well, we've seen Russia invade Ukraine 100 times in the past, and 5% of those times..." we can't dispute. In reality, I see the probability estimates we're providing as a way to improve the accuracy of our language. It's quite ambiguous to remark, "Oh, there's a fair possibility of things occurring" or "a significant likelihood." Whereas if I say, "Look, I give it 5% credibility," at least I'm stating my thoughts about the world. It is easier for us to communicate.

To play devil's advocate on artificial intelligence: Rodney Brooks, former director of MIT's Computer Science and Artificial Intelligence Laboratory, has said that we have no idea if general artificial intelligence will ever emerge. In a late 2017 post, he said that modern-day AGI research is not performing well at all on either being generic or sustaining an autonomous being with a continuous life. It appears to be stuck on the same reasoning and common-sense problems that AI has been grappling with for at least 50 years. All of the information I've seen indicates that we still have no clue how to make one. Its characteristics are completely unknown. " So, what assures you that you are not diverting resources away from needy people in the present in order to address an imagined threat?

I'd like to highlight two points. The first is simply that uncertainty is a two-edged sword. "Oh, we simply don't know how hard this is," Rodney Brooks adds, but this might indicate that achieving AGI is either easier or much harder. If you look at the history of technical forecasting, you will see that mistakes have been made in both directions. J.B.S. Haldane was a pioneering scientist of his day. In the 1920s, he predicted that a successful round-trip flight to the moon would take millions of years.

Second, the major laboratories are attempting to develop AGI. "When do you think it may happen?" you ask the folks who are creating it. When they say, "Well, 50-50 in the next 40 years," it seems rather confident to respond, "No, I simply believe it's quite near to zero."

And the quote you read is extremely amusing. This is often in AI, when people say, "Well, it can't even perform X," and then it accomplishes X. So, he claims that in 2017, AI has demonstrated no indication of generalizability. So now we have Gato, a good Deep

Mind model that can perform admirably in 60 distinct tasks. It's playing different games, moving robot hands, and chatting. We're already seeing the first indications of more broad systems. Similarly, contemporary language models are capable of a wide range of tasks. They can do basic algebra, basic programming, and basic conversational tasks such as questions and responses.

That remark also says that AI cannot do common sense thinking and so forth. Consider the LaMDA model once again. You may solve the following word problem for it: "A guy visits the most renowned museum in France's major city." While there, he notices the most renowned artwork, which reminds him of a cartoon he used to watch as a youngster. What is the nation of origin of the thing that this cartoon character is holding in his hand, in relation to the cartoon figure that he is thinking about? " And the AI answered, "The guy visited the Louvre in Paris." He saw the Mona Lisa, which was painted by Leonardo da Vinci, while touring the Louvre. Leonardo is also a Teenage Mutant Ninja Turtle's name. Leonardo, the Ninja Turtle, is holding a Japanese katana in his hand. "Japan is the solution."

"Okay, maybe AGI occurs, but how do we know it will be a major deal?" says the second half. So yet again, I'm thinking, "Maybe, maybe not. The key point I'd want to make is, "Man, we should be thinking about this." We need more than a handful of individuals focusing on possible issues, which is what we now have.

Longtermists aren't concerned with extending humanity's existence since they consider human reproduction as an aim in itself. Rather, the wellbeing of sentient creatures is the philosophy's measure of worth. Things that raise the sum of all subjective pleasure or decrease the sum of all subjective suffering are beneficial. As a result, extending humanity's existence is only beneficial from a longtermist standpoint if we believe that most people's lives include more well-being than misery, or that most people's lives are preferable to nonexistence. That seems to be something that cannot be confirmed. After all, none of us can say for certain what it's like to be dead. Nonexistence might be a joyful, egoless oneness with all creation—from which we are sadly, temporally banished for the duration of our human lifetimes.

Is it certain that I will not go to heaven once I die? NoI'm absolutely certain about almost nothing. But how shocked would I be? I'd be pleasantly pleased. Do I think it's more than 90% likely that there's no Heaven? Yes. I believe the arguments against heaven are compelling. The prevalent secular viewpoint is that being dead is equivalent to being unconscious. As a result, we experience nonexistence every night.

So let us agree that most human lives are preferable to nonexistence. According to your preliminary estimations based on survey responses and other data, 10 to 15% of the people on the planet would have been better off if they had never been born. If that's true, it's not clear to me why we should want humanity to last as long as possible.

One widely held moral belief is that our actions should be motivated by compassion for the less fortunate. Many children have been born and then abandoned throughout history, such that their only experience of life on Earth has been uncertainty, terror, and, inevitably, starvation. As a result, those babies would have been better off if the human race had never been. According to your utilitarian thinking, they would have been better off not existing. So where is the justice in asking them to suffer severe agony so that the rest of us may live our net-positive lives? Wouldn't a society that is ideal from the standpoint of the most despicable individuals be one in which humanity does not exist?

So here are two things: the first is that I reject Rawlsian notions of justice. Rawls holds the most radical viewpoint on the subject. He believes that it is reasonable to make the worst-off person in the world just a little bit happier at the risk of causing everyone else in the world to fall from heights of pleasure to a really awful situation. That is the exact meaning of his point of view. That is unacceptable to me.

Consider an asteroid approaching Earth and destroying everyone on the planet in 200 years. Assume that after 200 years, almost everyone will be living happy, prosperous lives. But one person will have a reasonably bad life and conclude, "Yep, on balance, I'd prefer not to have been born." Should we let an asteroid destroy the world? No, I don't believe so.

But, on a broader level, should we be particularly worried about lives marked by misery and the worst-case scenario? Yes, I think the answer is I think we should prioritize the avoidance of suffering above the promotion of pleasurable things.

Longtermists aren't only concerned with people's well-being. And, at one point in your book, you admit that the pain of factory-farmed animals may be so acute that it overshadows the positive well-being of all humans. If such is the case, it is unclear if increasing human longevity is a net-positive activity. After all, human consumption of factory-farmed meat has grown in lockstep with our species' diversity. If we assume that humanity will get wealthy in the future, there is a good chance that the ratio of unhappy factory-farmed animals to joyous humans will increase in the coming decades. Furthermore, if we construct sentient AIs and figure out how to maintain control over them, we may end up with billions of enslaved digital creatures in near-eternal torment. So, if we aren't even sure that prolonging humanity's existence isn't a net negative, why should we divert resources from alleviating the suffering of current people to avert our possible extinction in the future?

Yes, this irritates me greatly. And I think there is a strong argument for longtermists to favor trajectory change above extinction risk prevention. There is a wide range of opinions regarding the expected value of the future among the people I know. Some people are real optimists, believing that in the long term, we will just converge on the best state of affairs. In anticipation, I feel the future is lovely. People strive for pleasant outcomes. Sadists and psychopaths, for example, do not often maximize their chances of doing harm. More people wish to alleviate the suffering of factory-farm animals than want to purposely prolong their anguish. People want to eat meat; the discomfort is merely an unfortunate side effect. So, if we can manufacture meat in the lab in the future, those of us who care about animal welfare will advocate for it to be the only meat available. And the majority of people are unlikely to care.

So that is the process that leads me to believe that the future is favorably biased. However, I feel this is one of the large, hairy philosophical subjects on which I would want to see a lot more study done since it does have an effect on how you prioritize things.

Progressive political activists and effective altruists share comparable conceptual views. EAs, like left internationalists, oppose moral particularism and argue that all humans are morally equal. They, like many racial-justice activists, are concerned about being on "the wrong side of history." They, like socialists, aspire to use humanity's growing technological potential to build a future of universal human flourishing.

Importantly, they share a recruitment pool with today's left-wing social movements: EAs and progressive organisations both draw members from the community of idealistic college graduates.

You tried left-wing political activism before turning to effective charity. Why did you make that change? In a similar vein, why would you recommend a young person concerned about the global system's injustices and unfairness devote their limited funds and free time to EA rather than to, say, the DSA?

First, I'd want to point out that EA is not a monolithic movement with a diverse set of political ideals. But, speaking for myself, I came to effective altruism via left-wing causes. That was my first step. When I was younger and more worried about ethics, the first thing I did was vote for the Greens. And I fit the description perfectly: I thought The Guardian was too right-wing for me, so I got involved in left-wing politics. And I honestly see what I'm doing now, as well as effective altruism, as a continuation of progressive principles, which are essentially, look, you take equal consideration for everyone very seriously, with particular care for the disempowered and disadvantaged. That instantly motivates you to care about the world's impoverished, nonhuman animals, and people born in the next decades.

And then, secondly, well, what can we do about it? We essentially need to make some really tough decisions and partake in some pretty severe trade-offs. That, in my opinion, is what effective altruism is all about. It combines a moral approach that emphasizes impartiality—"All sentient beings matter"—with a focus on living with the reality that we cannot achieve everything. If I just choose my favorite charity, that is extremely unlikely to be the best way to contribute.

In fact, if a cause is now popular—if it's the problem that everyone in left-wing politics is focusing on—it's probably not the place where I can have the most influence. So, climate change is a huge problem, a huge task for the globe. But thankfully, we've had 50 years of work on it. And today, hundreds of billions of dollars are spent each year to combat it. With worst-case pandemics or AI, we're back to where we were with climate change in the 1960s.

Separately, a lot of social activity focuses on being dissatisfied or perplexed by the world's problems. From my perspective, it's more like, "Okay, I want to leave the world a better place than I found it. That is the primary cause. And you can always do that, no matter how bad the world is.

Opponents of effective altruism on the left have contended that questioning how you, as a person, can do the most good — in a really direct and immediate sense — breeds political pessimism. In an era when organized labor is disappearing and the global South is unable to mount a real challenge to the global order's inequities, it may be that the best thing any individual middle-class westerner can do for the world's poor is to contribute to competent organizations. However, this approach to change would merely alleviate the symptoms of global inequality rather than eradicate it entirely. At every given period in history, an individual seeking the greatest benefit for themselves will necessarily have to pursue change inside the present institutional framework, since no one person can hope to change that structure. However, really effective giving requires change on a scale that charity cannot hope to achieve. Making that kind of change requires a leap of faith that if I, as a person, devote myself to a radical movement for systemic change, others will follow-a leap that cannot be supported by facts.

Something about the critiques of EA makes me laugh: "You're overly focused on what you can measure," the argument goes in global health and development. "You must take this leap of faith." Then, in the long run, it's like, "What? You can't make any of this up. What about the proof? " And I say, "No. Look, there's this EA thinking spectrum. There are some who require actual evidence and end up in bed nets. Then there are those that want to go with whatever has the most value, and they tend to be long-termists. "

Right. To be clear, there are several mutually contradictory arguments coming from various groups of EA skeptics. But, if longtermists admit that we can't judge the most important things—and that there's significant value in even low-probability activities with a high payoff—why can't that reasoning justify seeking to foment, say, a global egalitarian revolution?

In theory, I guess long-termist logic applies there. It's just that people don't believe it. I do not speak for everyone in the movement. However, in my opinion, if you want to construct a socialist paradise, the most practical path to such a society is unquestionably via AI. In my lifetime, artificial general intelligence will completely reorganize society and allow for fundamentally new economic systems. That's what I'm assuming.

And right now, very few people are paying attention to it. That implies that a small person may have such a large impact. In contrast, if you say, "OK, I'm going to aim for a global communist revolution," a lot of people are already doing so. And you're up against a well-established political apparatus. So, I'm just more doubtful that it will work out. (Of course, there are other concerns about whether worldwide communist rule would be effective.) The track record is not stellar.

However, EA is not anti-political. It begins with an agnostic premise. We simply discover that different transformation tactics perform better in different areas. If we could make it happen, we all feel that supporting economic growth in disadvantaged countries would be preferable to supplying bed nets. But, in practice, what should we do? One option is to increase migration. And it's something that's been heavily funded.

But consider animal welfare. You may think that the best way to promote it is to encourage people to become vegetarians. However, it turns out that this has little impact. So, sure, maybe the best thing is to lobby governments. It turns out that the agribusiness lobby has gained such sway over the system that lawmakers are unable to intervene. So, in that scenario, corporate campaigning proved to be the best course of action.

In the event of pandemic preparedness, my best guess is that policy will be the most effective method. The best things you can support are projects that provide governments with more technical expertise and persuade those governments to take the issue more seriously. Forget about long-termism. Forget about respecting the lives of those living outside the United States. Even if we just consider threats to Americans in the next 30 years, the US government should devote much more resources to pandemic preparation.

So, the current issue is political. Today, no one in Congress is pressing for pandemic preparedness. Following 9/11, there were trillions of dollars in overseas interventions, as well as a new Department of Homeland Security. It's crickets after COVID. Nothing but nothing. There was this measure that would have authorized $70 billion in expenditure, which would still be less than a tenth of what the United States spends on the fight against terror. Nobody wanted to do it.

So just having the US government reflect the interests of its own people has a huge advantage in terms of pandemics. Influencing governments will far surpass any private initiatives on this subject. So, there is no ideological bias in favor of any one method of transformation.

HUMAN CIVILIZATION WILL CRUMBLE

A new paper claims that if we do not stop climate change now, human civilization will collapse by 2050.

The Chernobyl exclusion zone provides a picture of a lifeless world. According to a recent climate policy study, if humans do not act quickly to limit global warming, most of the Earth may look the same by 2050. (Photo courtesy of Shutterstock)

Every week, there's a terrifying new study about how man-made climate change will trigger the collapse of the world's ice sheets, the loss of up to 1 million animal species, and, as if that wasn't awful enough, make our beer very, very expensive. A new policy document released this week by an Australian think group asserts that the other assessments are somewhat wrong; the hazards of climate change are much, much worse than anybody can anticipate.

Climate change presents a "near-to mid-term existential danger to human civilization," according to the research, and there's a strong possibility society will collapse as soon as 2050 if major mitigation measures aren't implemented in the next decade.

The paper's central thesis is that climate scientists are too conservative in their predictions of how climate change will affect the planet in the near future, according to the Breakthrough National Centre for Climate Restoration in Melbourne (an independent think tank focused on climate policy). It was written by a climate researcher and a former fossil fuel executive. [Top 9 Possible Endings of the World]

Experts contend that the current climate crisis is bigger and more difficult than anything mankind has ever faced. General climate models, such as the one used by the United Nations' Panel on Climate Change (IPCC) in 2018 to predict that a 3.6-degree Fahrenheit (2 degree Celsius) increase in global temperature could put hundreds of millions of people at risk, fail to account for the sheer complexity of Earth's many interconnected geological processes, and thus fail to adequately predict the scale of the potential consequences. According to the experts, reality is likely to be much worse than any model can imagine.

How the world will end

So, what might a realistic worst-case scenario of the planet's climate-affected future look like? The authors illustrate one particularly bleak scenario in which world governments "politely reject" expert advice and people's desire to decarbonize the economy (find other energy sources), resulting in a global temperature increase of 5.4 °F (3 °C) by 2050. At this time, the world's ice sheets have disintegrated; catastrophic droughts have killed many of the trees in the Amazon rainforest, erasing one of the world's largest carbon offsets; and the globe has entered a feedback loop of ever-hotter, ever-deadlier conditions.

The authors suggest that 35 percent of the global land area and 55 percent of the global population are vulnerable to more than 20 days per year of lethal heat conditions, exceeding the threshold of human existence.

Meanwhile, droughts, floods, and wildfires wreak havoc on the nation on a regular basis. Desertification affects almost one-third of the world's land surface. Entire ecosystems are collapsing, beginning with the planet's coral reefs, rainforests, and Arctic ice sheets. The world's tropics have been hit the worst by these new climatic extremes, destroying crops and causing more than 1 billion people to flee.

This massive inflow of migrants, along with shrinking coastlines and drastic drops in food and water supplies, begins to strain the fabric of the world's main nations, including the United States. Armed clashes over resources are likely, maybe resulting in nuclear war.

According to the latest analysis, the end result is "outright anarchy" and potentially "the collapse of human global civilization as we know it."

How can this terrifying vision of the future be avoided? Only if the people of the globe see climate change as an emergency and start to work right now. According to the authors of the research, the human race has about a decade to launch a global movement to transition the global economy to a zero-carbon-emissions system. (Achieving zero-carbon emissions means either not producing any carbon or balancing carbon emissions with carbon removal.) The effort required would be "comparable in scope to World War II emergency mobilization," according to the authors.

Adm. Chris Barrie, a former Australian defense chief and senior royal navy commander who has spoken before the Australian Senate on the terrible potential of climate change for national security and general human well-being, wrote the foreword to the new policy paper.

"I warned the [Senate] Inquiry that, after nuclear war, human-caused global warming is the greatest threat to human survival on the planet," Barrie stated in the new report. "Human existence on Earth may be on the verge of annihilation in the most heinous way."

CHAPTER SEVEN

ACTUAL WAYS THE EARTH COULD END

Actual Ways the Earth Might End

The end of the world has arrived.

From catastrophic climate catastrophes to hostile aliens, Hollywood often portrays devastating endings to humanity's time on Earth.

For example, in the film "After Earth," which opens in theaters on Friday (May 31), a series of earthquakes, floods, tsunamis, and other natural disasters leave the planet unpleasant for humanity, forcing them to migrate to a new world called Nova Prime.

While the film may be pure fantasy, many scientists are worried about other catastrophic scenarios, some of which are considerably more terrifying than anything seen on the big screen.

1.Climate change

Climate change, the mother of all apocalyptic fears, is the most serious threat facing the world, according to many scientists. Climate change has the potential to exacerbate extreme weather, exacerbate droughts in specific areas, influence the distribution of animals and diseases around the world, and cause low-lying areas of the earth to flood as sea levels rise. The chain reaction of events might result in political instability, severe drought, malnutrition, ecological collapse, and other changes that make Earth a very unpleasant place to live.

2. It's an asteroid!

It's the stuff of disaster movies, yet scientists are scared that a cosmic asteroid will wipe out the planet. A meteor impact undoubtedly terminated the dinosaurs, and in the Tunguska event in 1908, a massive meteoroid damaged around 770 square miles (2,000 square kilometers) of Siberian woodland. Worryingly, scientists only know about a small percentage of the space rocks in our solar system.

3. Pandemic threat

Every year, new hazardous illnesses emerge: SARS (severe acute respiratory syndrome), avian flu, and, most recently, a coronavirus called MERS that originated in Saudi Arabia, have all been recent pandemics. And, because of our interconnected global economy, a deadly disease might spread like wildfire.

"The likelihood of a global epidemic is exceedingly worrisome," said Joseph Miller, co-author of the textbook "Biology" with Ken Miller (Prentice Hall, 2010). 2010 (Prentice Hall).

4. The presence of fungus in our midst

Though bacterial concerns are worrisome, fungal threats are even worse, according to David Wake, curator of the University of California, Berkeley's Museum of Vertebrate Zoology.

"We've seen a new amphibian fungal sickness that has truly had terrible consequences," Wake said of the chytrid fungus, which is wiping out frogs throughout the country.

A comparable fatal fungus in humans would be disastrous. While bacteria are dangerous, antibiotics are plentiful. Wake told LiveScience that we know a lot less about treating fungal diseases.

5. Disease modification

Natural ailments aren't the only ones to be concerned about.

The scientific community was outraged in 2011 when researchers created a mutant strain of the bird flu H5N1 that was transmissible in ferrets and spread via the air. The results raised concerns that diseases produced in the lab may escape from the lab by accident or design, resulting in a widespread pandemic.

6, Nunclear war.

Many scientists remain concerned about the conventional end-of-the-world threat: nuclear war. Aside from North Korean leader Kim Jong Un's threats and Iran's clandestine nuclear projects, massive stores of nuclear weapons across the globe might cause devastation if they fell into the wrong hands. The Bulletin of Atomic Scientists, a nontechnical periodical on global security founded in 1945 by experienced

Manhattan Project scientists, raised the Doomsday Clock to five minutes to midnight last year. The Doomsday Clock illustrates how close humanity is to extinction due to nuclear or biological weapons or a worldwide climatic disaster. [7 Surprising Cultural Facts About North Korea]

7. Robot ascension

Although "The Terminator" is science fiction, killer robots are not far from reality. The United Nations recently advocated for a ban on killer robots, ostensibly because experts were worried that several countries were developing them.

Many computer specialists feel that the singularity, the point at which artificial intelligence surpasses human intelligence, is near. It remains to be seen if such robots will be beneficial or a nuisance to humans. However, when hyperintelligent robots armed with lethal weapons are around, a lot may go wrong.

8. Overcrowding

Since the 18th century, when Thomas Malthus warned that population growth would cause worldwide starvation and overburden the globe, there has been widespread anxiety over an overpopulated Earth. With the global population at 7 billion and rising, many environmentalists believe population growth is one of the most serious threats to the planet. Of course, not everyone agrees; many believe that population growth will level out in the next 50 years and that society will innovate its way out of the negative consequences of any overcrowding.

The impact of a snowball

Though any of these scenarios is possible, most scientists feel a snowball effect of several incidents is more likely, according to Miller. For example, global warming may increase the prevalence of illnesses while also causing significant changes in the climate. Meanwhile, ecosystem collapse may make food production substantially more difficult, with fewer bees to fertilize crops and fewer trees to filter agricultural water. So, instead of an epic tragedy, several very small circumstances would gradually degrade life on Earth, Miller said.

In that scenario, Earth's extinction is "like getting attacked by a saber-toothed tiger," Miller told LiveScience. "It's more like being eaten alive by ducks."

The End

NOTE